W9-CCT-960

MASCOT

TO THE RESCUE!

MASCOT
TO THE RESCUE!

BY PETER DAVID
DRAWINGS BY COLLEEN DORAN

LAURA GERINGER BOOKS
An Imprint of HarperCollinsPublishers

Forest Park ES
Library

Mascot to the Rescue!

Text copyright © 2008 by Second Age, Inc.

Illustrations copyright © 2008 by Colleen Doran

All rights reserved. Printed in the United States of America.

No part of this book may be used or reproduced in any manner whatsoever without written permission except in the case of brief quotations embodied in critical articles and reviews. For information address HarperCollins Children's Books, a division of HarperCollins Publishers, 1350 Avenue of the Americas, New York, NY 10019.

www.harpercollinschildrens.com

Library of Congress Cataloging-in-Publication Data

David, Peter (Peter Allen)

Mascot to the rescue! / by Peter David ; drawings by Colleen Doran. — 1st ed.

p.   cm.

Summary: Twelve-year-old Josh, who feels connected to the comic book superhero Mascot, sets out on an odyssey to discover the comic's creator when he finds out that the fictional Mascot is going to die.

ISBN 978-0-06-134911-9 (trade bdg.)

ISBN 978-0-06-134913-3 (lib. bdg.)

1. Heroes—Fiction. 2. Cartoons and comics—Fiction. 3. Imagination—Fiction. 4. Single-parent families—Fiction.] I. Doran, Colleen, date, ill. II. Title.

PZ7.D28233Mas 2008   2007025906

[Fic]—dc22   CIP

                                                                                              AC

Typography by Carla Weise

1 2 3 4 5 6 7 8 9 10

First Edition

To the fans and their legendary sense of

humor about themselves . . . I hope

—P.A.D.

CONTENTS

CHAPTER 1

THE NEW KID IN SCHOOL

Kelsey Markus didn't know Mascot was going to rescue her that bright Monday afternoon. She was much too busy abandoning hope that things were going to be different at Demarest Elementary School to recognize a rescuer when she saw one. But as the first kid snickered at her, and then another and a third, she realized bitterly that she should have known nothing would change. It was going to be just like it was when she'd gone to Essex Elementary. She was starting over. She was "the new kid" again.

"Move it, lard butt," said one boy, shoving past her to get out onto the playground during recess. She staggered to one side, and then a crowd of boys came in from that side, pushing her the other way. "Beach ball!" called out one of them, generating even more laughter. The teachers tried to restore order, but the damage had been done.

Kelsey was fat. She knew that. They had mirrors around her house. She didn't make excuses for being over-weight. She loved to eat. It wasn't much more complicated than that. Some girls loved to eat and they never gained a pound, and no one made fun of them. So obviously (she reasoned) the whole eating thing wasn't really the prob-lem. It was the gaining part, and that was simply bad luck.

She didn't know how much she weighed. She'd stopped using a scale back in third grade. Instead Kelsey tried to focus on the important things: Her father and grand-parents and family all loved her. And she knew she was a good person. She was certain of it. So why should anything else matter?

Still . . . it was tough being the new kid in school, espe-cially since they were already well into the school year and she'd just moved into town. She wasn't stupid. She knew the harsh truth of things—a fat girl got made fun of, and no one wanted to be friends with someone who got made fun of—but she had been hoping that Demarest would be different somehow.

But no: same old, same old.

Kickball, tetherball, even an impromptu game of tag—she tried to join in but wasn't welcome. She could complain to the teachers, but what would be the point of that? Telling on other kids would squash any remote chance of making friends.

She would have loved it if once, *just once*, someone had needed her for a team.

"You goin' to the bake sale?"

She was sitting on the bottom rung of the jungle gym, her heels rocking back and forth on the ground. She looked up, and up, at the large boy who had addressed her. He looked short, but his chest and arms seemed pretty muscular.

Kelsey stopped rocking and studied the boy warily. She suspected he already knew the answer to the question; his asking it was simply a formality, part of an endless ritual of bullying with which she had become all too familiar. "Why?" she said guardedly.

"That means yes," the boy said smugly. He put out his hand. "Gimme the money y'got for it."

Automatically her hand went to her right hip pocket,

tipping him to precisely where she carried her money. The boy, whose name was Fred, saw the gesture and smiled the sort of cruel smile that only boys named Fred who are about to steal money could smile.

"Come on," he said. "It's not like skipping a meal is gonna kill you."

Several of Fred's pals came up behind him to watch the fun. They wanted to see the fat girl cry.

Kelsey closed her hand tightly on her pocket, trying to send Fred a clear signal that she was not going to be as easy as all that, and perhaps it would be best for him to back off. Strands of her thick, curly brown hair fell in front of her eyes and she pushed them aside, not wanting to break eye contact.

If he received the signal, he gave no sign. Instead, quickly glancing around—presumably to make certain no teachers were heading their way—Fred abruptly lunged for Kelsey, grabbing at her pocket.

Kelsey's weight actually gave her some advantage—she thrust forward and sent Fred staggering off balance. But she was at a bad angle, perched as she was on a rung of the jungle gym, and Fred had enough leverage to press his advantage.

That was when things suddenly became very strange.

"*Get your hands off her!*" came a loud, reedy cry.

Everybody looked up.

There on the branch of a large oak tree just above the jungle gym, perched like an eagle about to swoop, was a very thin boy. He had a shock of blond hair, a round face, and freckles. Most curiously, he had a domino mask drawn on his face across his eyes. Apparently he had used a black Magic Marker. He was sporting a blue Windbreaker and was gripping either side, stretching it out so he looked as if he had wings.

"I said get your hands off her!"

"*Make me!*"

The boy obliged, shouting, "Justiiiiice!" as he leaped into battle.

What Kelsey, Fred, and the assorted boys saw was a crudely masked boy in a tree, who was barking orders—or perhaps simply barking mad.

The young would-be hero, on the other hand, saw things very differently. This is what he saw:

The valiant Mascot, scourge of evildoers, pauses in his patrol of the city. A cry for help? It is like a beacon to him, summoning him to the rescue. From high atop a building, Mascot crouches upon a ledge

and spots a young woman in distress. Five massively
built thugs, each dressed in telltale costumes of
green and gray, surround her. Clearly they work for
the Humiliator, the scourge of Metaplex. Mascot
fumes over the sheer audacity of the Humiliator,
who apparently thinks he can get away with
whatever he wants. Well, Mascot will show him, you
can just bet he will.

Shouting his rallying cry of "Justiiiiice!" Mascot
leaps from the building ledge. The evil minions
barely have time to react before Mascot crashes into
them.

He sends them sprawling and bounces to his
feet like a jack-in-the-box. Without slowing down, he
charges the nearest of the thugs and hits him so
hard and so far that the bad guy leaves his shoes
behind as he goes flying. Mascot continues to move
like a blur, fists and feet everywhere. The bad guys
are begging for mercy.

Kelsey had been so startled by the boy's sudden arrival
that she had fallen back between the bars of the jungle gym
and landed heavily on the ground. She scrambled to her
feet just in time to see the masked boy drop from the tree

and land squarely on Fred.

Fred staggered from the impact, but he was far bigger and taller than the boy and so had little problem twisting quickly and sending the boy spilling to the ground. The impact ripped the boy's right trouser knee. He rolled and bounced to his feet, hands poised in a reasonable facsimile of a boxer's stance. "Hello, boys," he called out with boundless confidence as if he were not, in fact, outnumbered. "In case you've forgotten me, I'm Mascot . . . which means I'm good luck! But not for you!"

This prompted snickers from several of the boys. "Mascot" vaulted toward Fred once more. He covered half the distance, and then Fred brought his fist around in a slow arc and landed a punch squarely on Mascot's chin.

Mascot went down and Fred let out a yelp, not because Mascot had injured him, but because the bone-on-bone of his knuckles against Mascot's jaw hurt a lot. Mascot, meanwhile, didn't seem to register that he'd been hit. Instead he got to his feet and, grabbing one of the other boys by the shirtfront, managed to catch the boy by surprise.

That was as far as Mascot's luck carried him. Rallying over the indignity of being, albeit briefly, incommoded by a twerp with Magic Marker on his face, the boys converged on Mascot and proceeded to pummel him to the ground.

Kelsey tried to come to Mascot's aid, but the crossbars of the jungle gym blocked her. Unsure of how she had managed to slip in, she found herself unable to get back out. Her bulk was holding her prisoner. She started pushing her way through and got stuck halfway. So she watched helplessly as Mascot went down beneath his enemies' fists.

The most curious aspect of this already supremely strange sequence of events was that Mascot appeared oblivious to the thrashing. Instead he flailed away, connecting every so often with punches that had no power behind them, and he kept shouting, "Had enough? Oh, you want some more? There's plenty more where *that* came from!" as if he were actually winning.

Kelsey finally managed to pull herself out, falling on her face. Before she could intervene on Mascot's behalf, however, there was the sharp sound of a whistle slicing through the air. Coach Gaffney, who was playground monitor that day, sprinted across the school yard, running with his characteristically perfect precision of motion as he continued to blow his whistle.

Fred and his boys hotfooted it out of there as quickly

as they could, leaving Mascot flopping around like a beached carp. Mascot tried to stand, managed for a second or two, and then fell forward again. He shook his fist in impotent fury and shouted, "That's right, run! Run because you hear the police sirens, same as I do! But you tell the Humiliator this isn't over! Not by a long shot! Or my name isn't Mascot!"

"*Your name isn't Mascot!*" said the irritated Coach Gaffney, grabbing Mascot by the back of his shirt and hauling him to his feet. Gaffney's round and normally red face grew even redder as he studied the damage Mascot had sustained. He moaned as he saw the bloody nose, the scratches, and the lower lip that was beginning to swell. "Uh boy, look at those shiners!" he said. "I'm gonna hear about this. . . ."

Kelsey spoke up as she dusted herself off. "I think that's Magic Marker, actually."

Gaffney took a closer look and sighed impatiently. "Josh, for crying out loud, what did you do to yourself?"

"*They* did it to *him!*" Kelsey said in protest. "He was trying to help me—" She stopped, and a slow smile spread across her face because she couldn't recall the last time that had happened. "He was trying to help me," she repeated, hoping that Coach Gaffney would understand.

Mascot—or "Josh," as Gaffney had addressed him—said darkly, "The forces of evil are never ending."

"So is this nonsense with you. Come on. Let's get you to the school nurse, *again*." He started to walk, then stopped and called to Kelsey, "You too. Mrs. Farber is probably going to want to talk to you, find out what happened."

The name didn't mean anything to Kelsey, although she was pretty sure it wasn't the principal's name. She nodded and fell into step alongside Josh.

Other kids were approaching, curious, pointing and laughing. Gaffney waved them aside, threatening all manner of detentions and punishment for anyone who chose that moment to get in his way. As he did so, Kelsey saw that Josh was staring at her fixedly. "*What?*" she demanded, suddenly feeling even more self-conscious than she usually did.

"Of course," he said. "I'm an idiot." That much Kelsey could have told him from what she'd already observed, but then he lowered his voice and continued, "It's all right. Your secret identity is safe with me."

"My *what*?"

He put a finger to his lips, said, "Shhhh!" and then added so softly that she could barely hear him, "There are enemies everywhere. We'll talk later."

Of all the ways that Kelsey could have guessed her first day at school would go, this was one that had never occurred to her.

Forest Park ES
Library

CHAPTER 2

TERROR OF THE MISSTERMIND

Mascot, one of the two greatest heroes of Metaplex—next to Captain Major, of course—doesn't even bother to struggle in the chair that's holding him tightly bound. He glares defiantly at Misstermind and sneers. "Do your worst. Scrape out all my thoughts like ice cream with a spoon. I won't tell you anything, and just you wait until Captain Major comes bursting in here to rescue me. Then you'll see what's what."

Misstermind moans softly. She may be beautiful, but Mascot isn't the least bit moved by her charms. He knows she is the enemy, and however much she may try to dig her fingers into his brain, she's going to find that there's nothing there.

"I'm your friend, Josh," she tries to assure him.

A pathetic trick. She thinks that she has figured out his secret identity and is trying to trick him into confirming it. Fortunately, Captain Major has taught him well, and such obvious tactics aren't going to work. "Sorry, lady," he says icily. "I don't know any Josh."

Mrs. Farber leaned back in her chair, tilted her horn-rimmed glasses back up onto her head, and rubbed the bridge of her nose. "Josh . . . Josh, please . . . I know this is all a game to you."

"If fighting the forces of evil is a game," Josh said defiantly, "then call me the undefeated champ." He was sitting with his arms behind the back of the chair as if they were tied there.

The door to Mrs. Farber's office opened and a tired-looking woman with blond hair stuck her head in tentatively. There was an expression of knowing dread on her face. "Oh, Josh," she said with a groan, "what now?"

Mrs. Farber gestured for her to come in. "Thanks for coming over so quickly, Mrs. Miller."

"Well, when the school guidance counselor calls and says it's an emergency, how could I not?" She came around the chair and was now looking closely at Josh's face. "What did you do?" She drew her fingers across the top half of his face. "Why is it all red and sore around your eyes?"

"It's my mask," Josh told her. His voice had changed: There was none of the thundering bravado that had been present earlier. Now he just sounded like a nervous kid. "I mean . . . it was. . . ."

"He drew a mask on his face with Magic Marker," Mrs. Farber said, not sounding amused. "The nurse managed to wash it off with some heavy-duty soap. She tells me the rash should disappear in a day or so. He was playing super-hero again."

"Yes, I figured that out. But did you have to draw on those bruises too, Josh? People will think I'm the worst mother in the world."

"They're real," Josh said proudly.

His mother paled.

"He was actually," Mrs. Farber said with grudging

admiration, "somewhat heroic today. Some boys were picking on a girl and Josh came to her rescue. But," she added regretfully, "then the boys roughed him up."

"Oh, Josh." His mom sighed, touching his bruises tentatively. "How do you get yourself into these things?"

"She needed help," Josh said in a very small voice.

"Josh," said Mrs. Farber, "why don't you wait outside so I can talk to your mom for a few minutes?"

Josh nodded and went outside, closing the door behind him. His mom sank into the chair he had just vacated and shook her head.

"Mrs. Miller," began Mrs. Farber.

Josh's mom said, "Please. Call me Doris."

"All right . . . Doris."

Mrs. Farber was holding a pencil between her fingers, and she started tapping it on the top of her desk. "Doris, this business with Josh . . . it's been going on for some time now, hasn't it? This pretending to be a made-up superhero—"

"Oh, he's not made up," Doris told her. "Well . . . not by Josh, at any rate. It's a comic book. Here, look," and she pulled out from her large carrying bag a gaudy-looking magazine.

Mrs. Farber didn't pick it up. Instead she sort of cocked her head and looked at it sideways for a bit. "I see," she said, in that way that clearly meant she didn't really see at all. "And has he always had such an interest in these . . . things?"

"Much more so since his father left," said Doris, with that faint sigh she always gave whenever she mentioned the divorce. "He enjoys his comic books. He really gets into them."

"Perhaps . . . too much."

Doris raised her eyebrows. "What do you mean? It's harmless—"

"Harmless! Doris, he's jumping off tree branches, getting into fights, and calling himself Mascot. Aren't you at all concerned that he's losing track of what's real and what isn't?"

"No, I'm not," Doris said defensively. "What's so wonderful about the real world anyway? So many terrible things happen. At least he's reading! At least he's spending his time doing something other than hanging out on the internet, which"—and she raised a stern finger—"I don't let him anywhere near, just so you know."

"Yes, that's probably for the best. Doris . . . look," said Mrs. Farber. "I think Josh has some very serious issues, and it seems to me that you're not dealing with them."

"He's my son," Doris said, her back stiffening, "and I'll do what's right for him."

"And I am his guidance counselor, and I likewise have to do what I feel is right for him. This . . . fantasy life of his is a recurring problem, and I'm afraid I'm going to have to alert social services."

"*Social services?*" Josh's mom looked as if she'd been whacked in the face with a baseball bat. "That's who you go to in cases of child abuse! I'm not abusing him!"

"No, but you're not *dis*abusing him, either. Running around and pretending to be a superhero is unacceptable. Sooner or later he's going to get hurt."

"He's a good kid," Doris said, and then stood and added, "and I'm a good mother, and I'm doing my best."

"No one is saying you're not."

"Actually, I think that's exactly what you're saying," snapped Doris Miller, and she turned on her heel and headed for the door.

Mascot is busy using his hyperhearing to eavesdrop on the ranting of Misstermind. Thus far, it's been tricky to pick up. Perhaps Misstermind has some sort of white noise scrambling device that's making it difficult to—

"Hi."

Josh recognized Kelsey's voice instantly. Unfortunately, he had been leaning to the side of the chair he was sitting on, trying to hear better, and so wound up toppling off. He thudded to the floor.

"Are you all right, Josh?" Kelsey said.

"I'm fine. Fine," Josh assured her, bouncing to his feet

like a rubber ball. He squared his shoulders and put his hands on his hips.

Mascot smiles inwardly. Naturally he recognizes Large Lass, one of the founding members of the League of Extraordinary Justice. Her ability to manipulate her mass and become superheavy or superlight makes her one of the most powerful members of the group. The Leaguers all keep their identities private from one another, but certainly Large Lass is smart enough to know that he's recognized her.

The school secretary seated nearby was giving him strange looks. So he dropped his hands from his hips to look a little less heroic.

"I just—" She smiled shyly. "I just wanted to tell you that the way you jumped in with those boys . . . that was the bravest thing I've ever seen someone do . . . in person, I mean."

"It was no problem."

"And the way they ganged up on you . . . it wasn't fair." Her face darkened into a scowl. "I wanted to help you. I really did."

"It's okay. I know you could've knocked 'em around

really good if you'd had the chance."

She nodded and then stuck her hand out. "I'm Kelsey Markus."

Josh stared at her hand in confusion for a moment before realizing that he should shake it. He took it and shook it firmly, and said, "Josh Miller."

"I know. A lot of kids say you're crazy."

"Yeah? Like . . . how?"

"They say you think you're a superhero."

Josh paused, and then said cautiously, "Do you . . . like superheroes?"

"They're okay. I like them better when they're being their secret identities, though."

"Really?" He was still holding her hand in the handshake but had forgotten he was doing it. "But . . . but the superhero identity is so cool."

"I guess, but they're kind of . . . you know . . . bigger than life. I like my heroes life-size."

She smiled at him in a way that made him feel weird inside. That was when he realized they were still holding hands, and he quickly released hers as he shrugged and said, "Eh. Who cares what the other kids say, right? I mean, you don't care what other kids say about you, right?"

"Definitely right," she assured him. Kelsey stood there

looking a little uncertain. "Well . . . I'm going home now, I guess."

"Why?"

"Because school's over."

"Oh." Josh looked up at the clock. "Yeah, I guess it is."

"Well . . . I just . . ." She bobbed her head shyly. "Thanks again. . . . I . . . guess I'll see you around in school or some-thing—" and she couldn't resist adding—"hero."

She started to turn and walk out.

"Maybe you should—" Josh began.

Kelsey pivoted in place and looked at him. "Maybe I should what?"

Come over to my house, Large Lass. It might be nice to hang out.

Josh shrugged. "Be . . . more careful outside. During recess. I guess."

Slowly Kelsey nodded. "I . . . guess you're right." She sounded a bit confused, as if she knew that wasn't what he had wanted to say.

Josh's mother walked out of the guidance office and scowled down fiercely at Josh. If Josh had been able to read minds, he would have known that she was more annoyed with Mrs. Farber than she was with him, but Josh was sitting there and Mrs. Farber wasn't. "Let's go, Josh," she said irritably. She stuck out a hand. Josh took it tentatively and glanced nervously in Kelsey's direction.

That was when Kelsey spoke up: "Don't be mad at him, Mrs. Miller," she said, the words tumbling out of her mouth. "It was those other boys' fault, and not Josh at all, and he was really, really brave, and you shouldn't be mad at him for that."

"I don't think it's any of your business, young lady," Doris Miller said primly.

Kelsey didn't back down. "It kind of is, since I'm the one Josh got into the fight over. So it's my fault he got into trouble, and those boys' fault there was any trouble at all, so really, Josh is the last one who should be getting into trouble."

Mrs. Miller stared at her as if really seeing her for the first time, and then—to the surprise of both Josh and Kelsey—smiled. "What's your name?"

"Kelsey Markus."

"Are you new around here, Kelsey?"

Kelsey nodded.

"Hard to be the new girl in school," Mrs. Miller said. "My family moved around a lot when I was growing up, so it seemed like I was always the new kid. Never easy, is it?"

"No, ma'am. Anyway, I just wanted to say that I really thought Josh was very brave."

Doris looked her up and down, and her smile widened. "How long have you been friends with Josh?"

"Just since this afternoon."

"Oh!" Doris looked at her son. "So you just jumped in to help a total stranger, huh?"

"Mommmm," moaned Josh, and his cheeks turned red.

She turned her attention back to Kelsey. "Anytime you'd like to come over and visit, Kelsey, you're certainly welcome."

"*Mom!!!*" Josh's face colored even further, and he blew his cheeks in and out rapidly like a puffer fish.

"That would be nice . . . if it's okay with you, Josh."

Josh looked from Kelsey to his mother and then back to Kelsey again, and his shoulders slumped in something that Mascot would never have acknowledged possible: defeat.

"Whatever," he said, sighing.

CHAPTER 3

THE SECRET
STASH

*J*osh was seated cross-legged about five feet away
from the television, and he was aiming a plastic
gun at it. On the TV screen an assortment of monsters was
charging him, and he was calmly firing away. Electronic
bursts would appear on the screen in response to Josh's
marksmanship, and monsters were tumbling right, left,
and center. He wasn't thinking about the monsters,
though. He was thinking about Kelsey and the fact that she
was sitting next to him, watching wide-eyed.

"Wow. You're great. Do you ever miss?"

"I used to," Josh said, trying to sound casual. "But not for a long time now. I've gotten really good at this."

"Do you play any other video games?"

"A few."

Doris appeared, showing her amazing ability to say exactly the wrong thing at exactly the right time. "Why don't you show her your comic book collection?"

"Aw, Ma, she wouldn't care about that."

He was startled when Kelsey replied, "Yeah, I would. I like comic books."

This caught Josh completely flat-footed. "I thought you said you didn't like superheroes."

"No. I just like their secret identities better. It's . . ." She considered it. "It's hard to seem regular when you're super-special. It's nice of them, that they go to that much work."

"I never thought of it that way." Hiding his amazement, he laid down the gun, turned off the video game, went with her downstairs to the basement, and started hauling out his long, white boxes filled with meticulously bagged and indexed comic books. "Which heroes do you read about?"

She started flipping through the comics. "Where are your Archie comics?"

Josh sagged visibly. "I don't collect those. Girls collect those."

She looked at him pointedly.

"Oh. Right. You're a—"

"Girl?"

"Yeah. Pretty much."

"Well, sorry . . . I thought you read about superheroes."

"I do. I have."

He stared at her, confused. "You said you read Archies."

"Uh-huh. But they have superhero identities, too. Like Archie becomes Pureheart the Powerful, and Betty is Superteen, and Jughead turns into Captain Hero and Reggie is Evilheart—"

"Those stories don't count! Those are, like, imaginary stories. They're not *real*!"

She stared at him in disbelief. "Let me understand this. *My* superheroes *aren't* real . . . and yours *are*?"

Josh tried to respond to that but then just blew air out impatiently between his lips. "It's just different, okay? I thought you understood."

Seeing his disappointed look, Kelsey said gamely, "Okay, well . . . which one is *your* favorite? Maybe," she continued, "maybe I can try some of yours, and I'll lend you some of my Archies."

"We could do that," agreed Josh, who had absolutely no intention of reading any of her Archies, superteens or no.

Josh went straight to the back of the largest box. It was out of order alphabetically, but that didn't matter: He always kept this particular comic at the back so that he would be able to go straight to it at a moment's notice.

He extracted the precious comic with such delicacy that he might well have been handling a bomb. It was safe in its Mylar snug bag, and he held it up for her to see. Kelsey leaned forward and read aloud, "Captain Major #342: *The Origin of Mascot.*"

"Mascot wasn't always his sidekick. This is when he first showed up, two years ago."

"Can I read it?"

"*Read* it?" Josh echoed. The concept was strange to him. He'd read it so many times that he'd memorized every single word, could reproduce every drawing. He didn't need to read it anymore; he could experience it by just holding it. Obviously, though, Kelsey didn't share that ability and, well, she *was* trying.

"Okay, sure, I guess. Don't take it out of the bag . . . lemme do it," he said, and he eased the comic carefully out of its sleeve. "Are your hands clean?"

"You're the first boy I've ever met who worried about

clean hands," said Kelsey, amused. But to set his mind at ease, she went off and washed her hands. Having thoroughly dried them, she dropped onto the floor cross-legged and held out her hands side by side, palms up. He opened the comic for her and watched as she paged through.

The first thing to leap out at Kelsey was the name of Mascot's secret identity. "Josh Mills? His name is Josh Mills?" Josh nodded. "That's awfully close to Josh Miller," she said.

"It sure is. And that's not all." He began to talk quickly, excitedly, faster than Kelsey could possibly turn the pages to read it for herself. "Captain Major took Mascot on as his sidekick after Josh Mills's father mysteriously disappeared. And my father mysteriously disappeared just a few months before."

"He did?" Kelsey's eyes went wide.

"Yup. Oh . . . Mom tried to make it sound like the marriage broke up and he walked out on us. But I know she's just covering."

"Covering?"

"Uh-huh. Look, it's right there, on page eighteen, panels one through three."

Unsure of what she was going to find, Kelsey turned to

the page Josh had indicated. There was Captain Major, his hand resting on Mascot's shoulder, and he was saying:

Don't you worry, Mascot. I'm sure that if and when your father can return, he will. It could be anything keeping him away from you: Space aliens. A secret spy mission. You never know. But it's going to be hardest on your mother. You have to be the man of the house until he comes back.

"But . . . how would Captain Major know these things about Josh's dad?" said Kelsey, not entirely convinced.

"Ahhhhh," said Josh, waggling his finger as if she'd just hit upon a secret of the universe. "That's part of the mystery. Me, I'm thinking maybe Mascot's dad is really an operative for the Stellar Protection Alliance that Captain Major works for, and Captain Major swore to him that he'd watch out for Mascot while Mascot's dad was off on a dangerous mission. Or—and this one I like the best of all—I think Captain Major really *is* Mascot's dad, but he has to keep it a secret."

"Why would he have to keep it a secret?"

"Because that's what superheroes do. Keep secrets. Anyway, we've got almost the same name, and our dads both disappeared, and there's all sorts of other stuff. Like in issue three fifty-three, Mascot's mom goes out on a blind date with this guy who's nasty to her and then sticks her with the check in a restaurant, and it turns out he was actually a supervillain. The exact same thing happened to my mom, except he wasn't a supervillain. At least I don't think he was. Oh, and one month when Mascot's mom was out of work, the electric company cut off their power. Right around the same time, our phone got cut off because Mom couldn't pay the bill. It's, like, every couple issues stuff happens to both Mascot and me."

"So . . . what are you saying, Josh? That it's your life in this comic book?"

Josh shrugged. "I dunno. It's just . . . it happens a lot."

"Well, sure, it happens a lot, Josh, but that's all kinds of general stuff that can go wrong with any mom who's on her own and doesn't have a lot of money. Right?"

"Yeah. I guess."

Josh was suddenly sorry he'd brought it up.

Kelsey looked into Josh's eyes and saw disappointment crawling across them.

Without missing a beat, she said, "Although, you know, now that I think about it . . ."

"Yeah?" he prompted. "What?"

"Well . . . you could take one or maybe two things and say it was coincidence. But a whole bunch of things . . . that's very different, isn't it? I mean, the odds keep going up and up with each thing until you're left kind of wondering . . . maybe it's not coincidence."

"*Right!*"

"It's like . . . the two of you are sort of connected."

He pumped the air in triumph. "Wow! You're the first person to get that! And the way I figure it," he said, holding up the latest issue, "if Mascot can get through all the stuff that he has to deal with . . . then I can get through all of mine. He's just what his name says: He's my good-luck charm. If he can handle it, then so can I. As long as he can keep going, it . . ." His voice trailed off.

"It makes it easier for you to keep going?" she said gently.

Josh nodded. Much to his mortification, he felt a stinging in his eyes. The last thing he wanted to do was cry in front of a girl, especially one who seemed as cool as Kelsey. He rubbed his eyes as hard as he could.

"Are you okay, Josh?"

"Fine. I'm fine," he said.

Mascot remains concerned that Large Lass, being a girl, will blab news of his secret identity to the world.

He reminds himself, though, that she is a hero in her
own right, and heroes can always be trusted.

He forced a smile.

"Can I show you something," he said cautiously, "that
I've never shown anybody else?"

She looked at him sidelong, not entirely sure where this
was going. Cautiously she said, "Where do you keep it?"

"Here, in this box."

"Oh. Well . . . sure. I guess."

He reached in and pulled out a pad that was labeled
"Artist's Sketchbook." He handed it to her and she started
flipping through. There, leaping across the pages, was an
assortment of superheroes, meticulously drawn in pencil.

"Is it lousy?" he asked. "If it is, you can tell me. I can
take it."

She had a feeling that he, in fact, couldn't have taken it.
That it was his fear of someone telling him it was no good
that had prevented him from showing it to anybody else.
Fortunately she didn't have to lie.

"These are good, Josh. Really good," she said.

"You think?" He sighed with relief. "Wow. You're, like,
my new best friend."

"I am?" No one had ever said anything like that to her before.

"Yeah. Of course," he added, "it's not like I've ever had an *old* best friend. And . . . hey . . . you don't have to be my new best friend if, y'know, you don't want to, because . . ."

"No. No, it's fine," said Kelsey. At that moment she decided that there was no one in the world she wanted to make happy more than Josh Miller.

When the doorbell rang, Doris put aside the book she was reading and answered it. She was surprised to see a rather handsome man standing there. Not movie-star handsome, but . . . not bad. He had sandy hair and a tanned complexion that made him look as if he were outdoors quite a lot. He was dressed casually in a blue sweater with sleeves rolled up to the elbows, faded jeans, and sneakers. He was about half a head taller than she was.

"Hi. I'm Kelsey's dad," he said.

"I'm Josh's mom." She shook his hand and then smiled. "I remember when I used to have an actual name."

"Zack," he said, laughing.

"Doris."

"I'm here to pick up Kelsey."

She turned, cupped her hand to the side of her mouth and called, "Kelsey! Your dad's here to pick you up!" She turned back to him and said, "I would have driven her home. . . ."

"Oh." He waved off the notion. "I wouldn't have wanted you to go to the trouble. Where are they?"

"Down in the basement."

He frowned.

Down in the basement, Kelsey and Josh heard the doorbell, followed a minute later by Josh's mother calling, "Kelsey! Your dad's here to pick you up!"

"I thought you lived nearby," Josh said.

"I do." Kelsey sighed. "It's . . . well, it's just me and my dad, and he gets worried. I told him I'd walk home, but . . ." She tilted her head in a what-can-you-do? manner. Josh understood perfectly.

Josh and Kelsey trotted up the stairs from the basement, and as they did so, they heard a man's voice in the midst of saying, "—downstairs by themselves? Mrs. Miller, I can't say I'm thrilled about that. A boy and a girl together should have an adult with them at all times."

"At their age? What do you think could possibly happen?" Josh's mother sounded amused.

Kelsey's father didn't. "It's different for you. Your son is a boy."

"Most sons are."

"You know what I mean."

"Yes. You mean my son can't be trusted."

"I didn't say—"

Josh and Kelsey chose that moment to emerge from the basement. Kelsey's father looked relieved when he saw his daughter and held out a hand to her. "Time to go, Kelsey."

"Daaaaaaaaaaad," she said, dragging a one-syllable word into three. "Stop treating me like I'm a little kid."

"She's been saying that since she was a little kid," Kelsey's dad said to Josh's mom. "Well . . . thank you for having her over."

"It was our pleas—"

She didn't get to finish the word *pleasure* because Zack had already taken Kelsey firmly by the hand and was heading down the walk toward his car, parked in the driveway. Doris noticed that Zack was limping slightly.

Kelsey managed to get a wave off before her father ushered her into the car.

"Strange man," murmured Doris, and Josh had to agree.

* * *

Some time after Kelsey had left, and Josh had been forced to admit to himself and to his mother that he'd had a really good time with her, he overheard his mother talking on the phone in the kitchen. She said his name as he happened by, so he backed up and listened carefully, even though he knew he shouldn't.

He was pretty sure that his mother was talking to Mrs. Farber. His mom was being all defensive, and saying that she knew what was best for her son, and Josh just had an active imagination was all, so why not leave him alone, and he didn't need to start going to mental doctors to help him deal with his problems because he *was* dealing with his problems and they just didn't like the way he was doing it, and why couldn't they just keep their noses out of her and Josh's business and stop threatening them with social services, and she was a good mother and where did Mrs. Farber get off making her feel like she wasn't, and yes, that's exactly what she was doing, don't deny it, and she had nothing more to say, good-bye, click. (The click was the sound of the phone hanging up, which Josh—in his mind's eye—envisioned in comic book terms as **CLICK**.)

He thought he heard her gently crying then. He hated that. Seeing his mother cry always gave him a weird uneasy feeling in his stomach. "Mom?" he called softly.

He heard her snuffle quickly, trying to pull herself together, and she said, "If this is about dinner, honey, I haven't started—"

"No, it's not about dinner. Are you okay?"

She stuck her head out the kitchen door. "How long have you been standing there?"

He shrugged.

"What did you hear?"

Another shrug.

"Josh . . ." She stepped out of the kitchen and crouched to face him. Taking his face in her hands, she asked tentatively, "Are you . . . happy?"

"About what?"

"About . . . anything. Everything."

"Sure." It seemed a silly question to him.

"Are you positive?"

He still had no clear idea what they were talking about but decided that staying with the affirmative would be the best strategy. "Yeah."

"Good." She kissed him on the cheek and ruffled his hair. "What would you say to pizza tonight?"

"I'd say, 'Helllooooo, pizza.'"

CHAPTER 4

"IN THE NEXT
SHOCKING ISSUE . . .'

Josh lived for the first Wednesday of each month, because that was when his subscription copy of the latest *Captain Major* arrived. The mailman—mailwoman, actually, in Josh's case—knew better than to bend the flat package containing Josh's comic and try to shove it into the Millers' mailbox. Instead she would always ring the doorbell in the morning (they had a fairly early morning mail delivery) and place the package reverently in Josh's eagerly awaiting hands.

Josh would then rush with it to the breakfast table, carefully unwrap it, and eat his cereal with one hand while turning the pages with the other. On *Captain Major* days he refused to pour milk into his cereal, preferring to eat it dry rather than risk dripping anything on the precious pages.

Doris was sleeping in. She'd been up until all hours the previous night, working a party for one of her clients. Doris earned a living cleaning other people's houses in one of the wealthier sections of town, and occasionally she'd pick up additional money by serving drinks at parties or working in the kitchen. Josh had woken up when he heard the front door close and glanced at the glowing numbers on his digital clock: It read half past two. Josh shook his head. Adults were so strange, having late parties on school nights.

So it happened that Josh was by himself when he read the story line that would radically reshape his life. Slowly, as he turned each page, his spoon began to shake more and more, until it was trembling so violently that the Cheerios went skittering. He felt a distant thudding in his forehead, and three quarters of the way through he had to turn back to the cover to make certain that this was indeed the latest issue of *Captain Major* and not some other title that had been delivered by mistake.

By the time he got to the final, horrifying end, he felt a lump in his throat that he would have been certain was stuck cereal, except that he had stopped eating six pages earlier. He wanted to go running to his mother, to have her read it, to have her assure him that it couldn't be true, that it was all just a terrible, awful mistake. He ran upstairs, the comic clutched in his shaking hands. Peering in through the open doorway to her bedroom, though, he saw her sleeping, wrapped in a blue fuzzy blanket. She looked so peaceful that he couldn't bring himself to wake her.

So, violently stuffing the comic into his backpack, Josh headed off to school like a sleepwalker. It was a measure of just how upset he was that he didn't take care to first put the comic into a Mylar snug bag with a cardboard backing.

The first half of the school day was a blur. Josh was ready when called upon and answered all questions when asked. But he didn't remember a moment of it. He was functioning entirely on autopilot.

When recess came, Josh was even more isolated than usual. He took himself off to a tree at the far end of the grounds, slumped against the trunk, and just stared off into space. He was so out of it, he wasn't aware that Kelsey had come over to him until she said his name very loudly right in his face and clapped her hands. He stared up at her, and it took his eyes a moment to focus. "Oh. Hi," he said listlessly.

"Josh, what *happened*?"

Josh and Kelsey had been hanging out for the better part of a month. As much as Josh would have been loath to admit it, she really wasn't bad for a girl. She had continued to try to sell him on the joys of Archie comics, and he'd done his best to seem interested. More important, though, their friendship had actually moved beyond comics into the arena of video games. It turned out that Kelsey was a devastating Forbidden Dragon Realm IV player, and various situations within the game that had been thwarting Josh as a single player had melted when Kelsey had teamed up with him.

Now he stared up at her lifelessly, as if all the joy had left him forever. "Josh," said Kelsey with growing concern, "what is it? Is something wrong with your mom?"

"Worse," he said tonelessly.

"Well . . . what?"

Without a word, he reached into his backpack and withdrew the comic. Kelsey's eyes widened in shock. She immediately noted the less-than-mint condition and knew it was out of character for Josh to treat one of his precious comics that way.

Clearly something truly horrific had transpired between the covers of the latest issue of *Captain Major*. She made a mental note of the fact that Josh considered something happening in a comic book to be more earth-shattering than something happening to his mother, but she supposed she shouldn't be surprised by that.

"Josh . . . ?" She knew she didn't have to prompt him much. He needed someone to talk to, and she was obviously that person.

"They're criminals," he said.

"What?" She stared at him, uncomprehending. "What are you talking about?"

"Captain Major . . . it's . . ." He was having trouble putting the words together. "The whole comic's changed. Captain Major . . . it turns out that in the past, before he became a superhero . . . the whole reason he became a superhero . . . was because he killed people."

"*What?*"

"A lot of people. It . . ." He was shaking his head, and all the blood was draining from his face. "It turns out that he used to work for the Mob. He killed people for the Mob."

"You mean he was a hit man?"

"Right. His real name was Butch Longo. And then he

was assigned to kill this guy who owed the Mob money, and it turned out the guy was actually his brother, and so he turned around and killed the Mob guys he worked for and then created this whole new identity for himself, the identity of Bruce Lance, which has always been his secret identity as Captain Major. But now his identity has been revealed—"

"Revealed? You mean everybody now knows that Bruce Lance is Captain Major?" Kelsey was stunned. A superhero's secret identity was always kept under wraps. No matter what.

"Yes. And now the police are after him because of what he did as Butch Longo, and the Mob has sent a squad of killer ninjas after him. Everything's changed in one issue . . . everything. It doesn't read like the same comic anymore. And now the Captain and Mascot are on the run, but that's not the worst part."

"It gets worse? How could it possibly get worse?"

Without a word he flipped to the back of the comic and held it up for her. She looked at the last page and could scarcely believe what she was reading.

"'In the next shocking issue . . . because you demanded it . . . the death of Mascot'? What does that mean? Because who demanded it?"

"I don't know. I don't know who 'you' is."

"Well, we've got to find out."

"How?"

"On the internet. That's how you find out everything."

"My mother doesn't let me go on the internet."

"Why not?"

"Because she says it's filled with sick, stupid people."

Kelsey frowned. "How would she know?"

"She goes on the internet all the time."

"So do I."

"She even keeps a regular, like, diary. . . ."

"You mean a blog."

"Yeah."

"Okay, so . . . if I'm on the internet and so is your mother . . . wouldn't that make your mom and me sick, stupid people?"

Josh's mouth opened to reply but then closed. "I dunno."

"Look . . . after school, come over to my house. We'll go on my computer and we'll see what's going on, okay?"

Hope began flooding into Josh, providing some light in a sea of darkness. "Yeah. Yeah, okay. Sure." Then he frowned. "Are you sure I can come over? Your dad . . . I don't think he likes me much."

"Aw"—and she waved it off—"that's just him talking tough. He's not as bad as you think."

"So he'll be okay with my being at your house?"

"Oh, heck no. But we'll sneak you in. It'll be fine." She smiled. "Trust me."

Josh trusted Kelsey. He did. But somehow he didn't think it was going to be fine.

Getting Josh into Kelsey's house wasn't that big a challenge since Kelsey's dad wasn't there. "That's why he doesn't want me having you over after school. It's because he's not home," Kelsey explained. "He's at work."

"What does he do?"

"He's a police officer."

Josh began to feel a buzz in the back of his skull.

Mascot's danger sense goes off. The police, once the allies of Captain Major and Mascot, are now after them. Yet in order to determine the truth of the charges leveled against them, Mascot has to penetrate deep into the heart of enemy territory.

His pulse pounds furiously as he contemplates the terrible risk should he be caught. Can he and Large Lass, his unwilling ally, possibly elude the—

"Josh!"

"What?"

"You were just staring off into space. Are you okay?"

"Fine. I'm fine."

She shook her head in wonder. "You are so strange," she said. Then she gestured for him to follow and headed up the stairs to her room. He followed, glancing around to make sure that neither police officers nor ninjas were ready to leap out of the woodwork at him.

Kelsey's room was painted in cheery blues and yellows. There were posters around of various pop singers, none of whom Josh recognized. Her bed was neatly made, which impressed Josh since he couldn't remember the last time he'd made his bed. It always seemed kind of pointless to him: Why make it when by bedtime you're just going to mess it up again?

Kelsey's computer was already up and running. Slinging her backpack onto her bed, she sat down and started typing away.

"What are we looking for?" he asked.

"A comic book discussion board."

"A discussion board?"

"It's like a big public bulletin board where people get together and talk about whatever." She glanced over at him.

"How can you not know that? I thought everybody knew that."

It took her a few minutes of poking around before she finally found something called www.comicnewsforum.com. Josh was amazed as images from various pages appeared on the screen, interspersed with what appeared to be news items about comics.

"Hold on," Kelsey said. "I'm running a search for threads about Mascot."

Moments later a dozen threads with "Mascot" in the header appeared.

They started reading.

It took ten minutes to get the gist of it.

They read in silence, but the entire time Josh felt as if he were standing in a pit of quicksand and sinking slowly, slowly, down.

"They hate me," he said in dazed astonishment.

"You? Josh, they don't even know you. If they knew you like I know you, they'd really like you."

The nature of her compliment went right past Josh. "They hate him," he amended. "They hate Mascot. Everybody hates him. I don't . . . it's . . . did you see the things they said?"

She nodded grimly.

Josh pulled himself to his feet and faced the screen, leaning forward so he could see it better. He read from one post: "'Mascot was just a lame, desperate device that was stuck in by Stan Kirby two years ago to try and pump some juice into an outdated, over-the-hill comic book. They can't kill Mascot off soon enough for me.'" He scrolled to another comment and kept reading: "'This bold new direction for Captain Major has been too long in coming. It's probably going to be lousy, but at least props to them for listening to us and knocking off the lame boy sidekick.'" He turned to Kelsey and said, "What do they mean, 'listening to us'? What's he talking about?"

"Let's keep looking," she told him.

She tapped away on the keyboard.

"Okay," she finally said. "Okay, what it looks like is that they had a contest online. Readers could write in to decide whether or not Mascot should be killed off in the course of this new upcoming story line. They voted overwhelmingly for him to die. There's even . . . wow," she said. "They leaked the pages."

"What do you mean?"

"Here. Look."

Josh screamed and stumbled backward, his hands waving about as if he could knock the picture out of his head.

"*Get it away! Get it away!*"

"*Josh!*"

He hit the floor, trembling violently, and this time when his eyes stung, he made no effort to keep the tears back. "I'm going to die . . . I'm going to die. . . ."

"Josh!" Kelsey was shaking him, trying to get his attention.

"I'm going to fall off a bridge and die—"

"Josh, you're not him! You're not Mascot!"

"I *know* that!" Josh said. "But everything that happens to him happens to me, too! You can't deny that!"

"Sure I can! He's a comic book character! You're real!"

"But we keep having the same things happening to the both of us!"

"It doesn't make any sense!"

"It doesn't *have* to make sense! It's a *comic book*!"

Kelsey shook her head helplessly, unsure of how to respond. Finally she said, "We don't know for sure that he dies. That's where the sequence ends; maybe in the next pages, he survives somehow."

"And I'm supposed to . . . what? Keep my fingers

crossed that that's what happens? What if he doesn't? What do you say then?"

"'Whoops?'" she suggested. When she saw that he was retreating into himself—and not knowing what else to do—she went back to the comic book board and started reading other threads. Josh just sat there. The initial trembling that had seized him wore off, but he still remained seated with his knees pulled up to his face and his chin resting on them, his arms hugging his legs.

"This is unbelievable," she said after a while. "I'm looking at these other threads about other comics . . . and the guys here are complaining about everything. *Everything.*"

"What do you mean, everything?"

Kelsey was relieved that Josh had spoken at all. Deciding she shouldn't make too big a deal over it, she said, "Well, not *everything.* I mean, some of these threads are pretty okay. Just talking about stuff that's happened or that's coming up. There's a couple about who could beat who in a fight. And here's a long one about football, for some reason. But a lot of these guys . . . they just complain. They complain about writers and artists and characters and stories. They complain about the prices of comics, about how there's not enough of one kind and too many of another. They're complaining about their LCS . . . what's an

LCS?" Josh shrugged. She went back to the boards. "It's just . . . I mean, it's incredible. These are comics fans? I thought fans of stuff were supposed to be people who liked something. I'm a fan of all these guys"—and she pointed to her posters. "I buy their CDs and listen to their music. That's what makes me a fan. If I stop liking their music, then I'm not a fan anymore. I don't get how some guys keep reading comics and keep hating them but keep calling themselves fans. It just . . . it doesn't make any sense."

"Nothing makes sense anymore," Josh said bleakly.

That evening Kelsey and her dad were watching the local news on television and, to Kelsey's surprise, a picture of Mascot appeared on the screen. The TV reporter was named Alan Jackson. He was young, with a ruddy complexion and a mop of thick blond hair.

"A dirty secret that I have to admit to you viewers," said Jackson. "This reporter is a longtime comics buff, and I'm sad to report that comic book fans are reeling over the announced impending death of Mascot. Yes, the beloved sidekick is slated to die in next month's issue of *Captain Major*, condemned to death by fan voting."

Ten minutes later there was a knock at Kelsey's front door. She answered it and was astounded to see Josh standing there. He was out of breath. Apparently he'd run all the way from his house.

"Josh, what are you doing here?" Her father was down in the basement doing laundry. Even so, she dropped her voice to a whisper. "I'm not allowed to have friends over on a school night. . . ."

"Or get phone calls after eight—yeah, I know. Your dad's gotta lighten up." He took a breath and continued, "On channel twelve they had a—"

"I saw it."

"I've got to stop it."

"Stop it? Stop what?"

There was something very different in his demeanor. His shoulders were squared, his eyes blazing with determination. His hands were on his hips, elbows outthrust, and his jaw was sticking upward slightly. "I'm going to stop it from happening. I'm going to make certain that Mascot lives."

The dreaded Auracle, the terrifying computer entity that shows future events, spurs Mascot into action. He has seen a depressing, bleak future with him and the Captain on the run and under the gun. He has seen his own death. But if the Auracle thinks that

he, Mascot, is going to be deterred by such dire
prognostications, then the Auracle has another think
coming. Mascot is not one to be cowed by talk of
doomsday. No, Mascot will be the captain of his
own future, and—

"Josh!"

Josh blinked and looked at her. "I'm going to stop them. I'll make the publisher just . . . just not do it."

"You can't, Josh. You're just one kid."

"Yes. I can." He took her hand firmly in his and said, "And you're going to help me."

"No way. My dad will kill me."

"Kelsey"—there was something in his voice that hadn't been there before—"I . . . look, I can't do this without you. It's too big. It's . . . I need you," he admitted with a huge sigh. "I need you on my team."

He needed her. On his team.

"Sure," said Kelsey.

CHAPTER 5

INSIDE THE HOME OF DREAMS

Paul Tinker worked in the Home of Dreams.

It wasn't really his home, or anybody's home. Instead it was an office building at Park Avenue South and East 27th Street in the heart of New York City.

And no one was really allowed to dream there. Paul knew this all too well, because on those occasions when he had dozed off and started dreaming, he'd been angrily shaken awake by Joe Rotone, the gray-haired man who was head of the mailroom and also Paul's boss.

"Blast it, Paul!" Joe would snap at him, and Paul would jump to his feet. "Stop dreaming on the job!"

When Paul had been a kid, other kids had made fun of him and called him names like "dummy" and "retard." That had lasted until middle school, when he'd started growing and hadn't stopped until he was over six feet tall. His newfound height and great strength had put an end to the teasing. Until he got this job working for Joe.

Paul worked at Wonder Comics, the world's greatest comic book publisher. Someone had long ago nicknamed Wonder Comics the Home of Dreams, because each of its comics represented the dreams of one creator or another. The nickname had stuck.

This particular day Paul was rousted from his nap by Joe and was apologetic as always. Joe pointed across the mailroom at stacks of comics waiting to be distributed to various editors. New Wonder Comics titles came out once a week, and one of Paul's jobs was to sort them, bind them up with rubber bands, and bring them around to everyone who was supposed to receive them.

Paul dutifully got the stacks of comics together and piled them onto the mail cart. Then he pushed the cart out of the mailroom on the ninth floor and waited for the freight elevator that would take him up to the tenth floor, where all the editorial guys had their offices.

When the elevator doors slid open, he blinked in surprise.

There were two kids standing there, a boy and a girl. The girl was kind of chubby and was wearing a long red coat and a kerchief. The boy wasn't chubby and had a blue Windbreaker.

"Hullo," Paul said, and wheeled the cart in. The boy and girl stepped to either side to make room for him. The large freight elevator was kind of old and so made all sorts of noise as it rattled and shook its way up one floor. When the doors opened on the tenth floor, Paul pushed the cart out and was mildly confused to see the two kids follow him. The door to get in was activated by a plastic security card key so that intruders couldn't just come strolling in. Paul kept his dangling on a cloth lanyard around his neck. He saw that the kids were waiting for him to slide his card through the mechanism that would unlock the door.

"Hullo," he said again.

"Hello," said the girl. The boy waved halfheartedly.

Paul had no clue why these two kids might be here. "Are you with a tour?" he asked.

The girl and boy looked at each other, and then the girl

quickly said, "Yes. We are."

"But we got separated," the boy said.

"And we're afraid we're going to get into trouble," the girl added.

"Oh! Well, okay! Let's get you inside." He slid the card key through, and the door lock buzzed. The boy and girl entered quickly while he held the door open for them.

Paul turned his back to them as he eased himself backward through the door, pulling the cart carefully. Once he was through, he let the door swing shut and then turned back to the kids.

They were gone.

"Oh well," Paul said with a shrug and, confident that the kids would manage to hook up with their group, started making his rounds.

Luck had finally favored Josh and Kelsey, although initially matters had not been promising. When they had first arrived at the main entrance on the tenth floor, a formidable receptionist had been waiting.

"Hi," Josh had said gamely. "We're here to see Mr. Stan Kirby, the creator of Captain Major."

The receptionist had glanced over the top of her glasses. "Who are you two?"

"We're fans," Kelsey had said.

"And I really need to talk to him," said Josh. "It's urgent. It's a matter of life and death. I tried calling here, but all I got was voice mail. I couldn't get a real person. But you're a real person, right?" Josh added what he thought was a winning smile.

"I'm sorry," the receptionist had said firmly. "But you can't just show up out of the blue and expect to see a famous man like Stan Kirby. Where are your parents, anyway?"

"They're downstairs," Kelsey had told her quickly, firing a warning glance at Josh.

"Well, you bring them up here and I'll be happy to explain our policies to them," the receptionist had said.

Their heads bobbing in unison, Kelsey and Josh had grabbed the down elevator and returned to the lobby. Once there, Josh had said, "We have to find the freight elevator."

Kelsey had nodded and followed Josh out of the building and around the corner. There they'd found something marked SERVICE ENTRANCE. Josh had walked in with confidence and she had followed. They'd found the freight elevator, and that was how they came to encounter Paul on the way up to the back entrance of Wonder Comics.

Once inside, they made their way quickly through the corridors. It was lunchtime and most of the editorial staff were not around.

But it was kind of exciting to be there. Josh took in the giant posters of various Wonder Comics heroes and heroines all over the walls, not to mention the occasional free-standing cardboard cutout. And some of the cubicles and offices they passed were decorated with toys, mini statues, and action figures of Wonder's acclaimed superheroes.

On the other hand, Josh couldn't help but find it kind of disappointing. The comic book trappings couldn't really overcome the fact that, well . . . this place was a place of business. Offices were offices, no matter how many toys they might be crammed with. He voiced his disappointment to Kelsey, who looked at him oddly and said, "What did you expect?"

"I don't know. Moving walls. Sliding bookcases. Gigantic pennies and dinosaurs and maybe a huge wall filled with screens showing all sorts of places where crimes were happening."

Kelsey shook her head. "You're something else, Josh. I just haven't figured out what that is yet."

"Come on," he said.

Kelsey's impulse was to slink around the office and try

to avoid anyone seeing them. But Josh walked boldly, look-ing as if he owned the joint. The effectiveness of his approach became clear to Kelsey on the occasions when they passed people who actually worked there. Josh would nod, say, "Hi there," even toss off a confident salute. The adults would smile and nod and go on about their busi-ness, which made Kelsey realize for the first time that it was possible to get away with just about anything if you looked like you knew what you were doing.

Mascot walks the Hall of Heroes, brimming with con-fidence. This place of justice is where he belongs. He has finally come home.

Josh kept glancing over toward Kelsey for reinforce-ment, and she kept nodding approval. He found, much to his surprise, that he kind of liked showing off for her. It made him feel, in real life, a little like he felt when he was living in his own mind.

He moved past office after office. All of them displayed the names of the people who worked there, and he kept looking for Stan Kirby's name. But he wasn't finding it. He didn't recognize any of the other names, mostly because they were the names of editors, and who paid attention to those? His annoyance slowly began to transform into frustration and finally concern when he realized that he and Kelsey had circled the entire office and still hadn't found Kirby.

"Maybe his office is on another floor," suggested Kelsey.

"Maybe. But how're we going to get to the next—?"

"Who are you looking for?"

Both Kelsey and Josh jumped and let out startled yelps. That guy from the mailroom was standing a few feet away, looking at them quizzically like an oversize dog.

"We're . . . uh . . ." Josh was thrown for a moment, and then he drew himself up and cleared his throat. "We're looking for Stan Kirby."

"He's not here."

"Do you know when he'll be back?" said Kelsey.

The young man was continuing to look at them. "I'm Paul," he said abruptly, and held out a hand.

Josh shook it firmly. "Josh. This is Kelsey." She followed suit.

Paul released Kelsey's hand, and there seemed to be gears turning in his head. "You guys aren't with a tour, are you?" he said finally.

The two youngsters exchanged looks. Kelsey shrugged, unsure of what to say or do. "No," Josh admitted. "We just need to find Stan Kirby."

"How come?"

"Well," Josh began, "it's . . . kind of a personal matter that—"

"He's Mascot," Kelsey said.

Josh looked poison in her direction.

Paul appeared confused. "He is?"

"He thinks he is. Or at least he thinks that everything that happens to Mascot is going to happen to him, too. And since Mascot's getting killed in the next issue, Josh is worried he's going to die, too."

"Whoa." Paul took all of this in and then said, "Wow. That stinks. So you want to try and stop it, huh?"

"Yeah. We do," said Josh. "Can you help us?"

"Sure. I'll help you."

"Great!" Josh said, his spirits buoyed. "So if you could just tell us which floor Stan Kirby is on . . ."

"He's not on a floor. Not here. He lives out in Northchester."

Josh sagged against the wall, like a balloon running out of air. But he recovered quickly. "Do you have a phone number for him?"

Paul shook his head. "He doesn't have a phone."

"Well . . . what's his address?"

"I can't tell you that."

"Why?" Josh was trying to keep desperation out of his voice. "You know it's a matter of life and death."

"Yeah, but I'm not allowed."

"Just this once . . ."

"No," Paul said, and although his voice never wavered from its soft, gentle manner, there was also a no-nonsense tone to it. "I'm not allowed to give out addresses. Not of anybody. I promised I never would. I don't break promises."

"Well, you said you'd help Josh," Kelsey pointed out. "That's a promise, too. Are you going to break that promise?"

That brought Paul to a halt. His brow furrowed as he tried to determine the best way to proceed, and then his face cleared. "I'll take you," he said.

Paul pushed the mail cart into the mailroom, then picked up Stan Kirby's bundle of comics and cleared out his in-box crammed with fan mail. He carefully placed it all in a canvas bag. Joe, seated at his desk doing paperwork, watched him with confusion. "What are you doing, Paul?" he asked.

"I'm going to bring Mr. Kirby his fan mail and comics."

"You usually don't do that until the end of the month."

Paul shrugged. "It was kind of piling up, and it's a nice day, so I figured . . . unless you think I shouldn't. . . ."

"No, no," Joe said, shooing Paul away. "Go ahead. It's no big deal."

"Thanks, Joe."

Joe went back to his paperwork and didn't even glance up as Paul slung the bag over his shoulder and headed out the back door of the mailroom.

CHAPTER 6

MEANWHILE, BACK HOME . . .

Zack Markus, Kelsey's father, worked only three days a week, so he happened to be at home when the phone rang. He answered it with his customary, curt "Yeah?"

"Mr. Markus? This is Mrs. Farber at the school. I'm calling regarding Kelsey's absence today. It's just a customary follow-up to make sure that—"

"Wait, wait." Zack had been standing, but his right hip was starting to hurt him. He glanced in annoyance at the cane that stood upright in the corner. It was almost as if it were laughing at him. He hated using it, just hated it. He settled down in the chair next to the phone and said, "What do you mean, 'absence'? She's on a class trip today."

"A class trip?" The woman on the phone sounded puzzled. He could hear her shuffling some papers and then said, "Um . . . no. No, there's nothing about that. She's not on any class trip. Are you saying she's not there?"

"No, she's not here."

"Mr. Markus," said Mrs. Farber, her voice becoming stern, "if she's cutting school, that's a very serious infraction."

"You're telling me that my daughter has gone missing," replied Zack sharply. "She gave me a permission slip to sign. I signed off on it. Now you're saying that . . . what? She faked it? Lady, I don't know who you are, but if what you're telling me is true, then I've got more serious things on my mind than school infractions. Who else is absent today?"

"Mr. Markus, that's privileged information, and I can't—"

"The Miller boy. What's his name . . . Josh. Is he out?"

There was dead silence on the other end of the line for a moment, and then she said slowly, "As a matter of fact . . ."

"I knew it," snapped Zack. "I knew that kid was nothing

but trouble. I'll handle this."

He hung up even as he heard her starting to say something more. Getting up from the chair, he turned quickly, and suddenly his right hip started to give out on him. He caught himself on the edge of the chair and groaned in frustration. Then he limped over to where the cane was propped against the wall, grabbed it, and used it to propel himself up the stairs to Kelsey's room.

Her computer was on. Typical. She always left it on. He went straight to her Word file and called up what she'd recently been working on.

He found the file for the fake permission slip that she had generated. He shook his head, quiet fury building, and then he did some more checking around. It took him no time to find her private journal.

He didn't have to read far.

Doris Miller staggered into the kitchen with an armload of groceries and saw that the message light was blinking on her phone. She muscled the bags onto the table, walked over, and pressed the play button.

"Mrs. Miller," came a familiar voice that prompted Doris to flinch upon hearing it. "This is Mrs. Farber from the school, and I believe we have a very serious problem with—"

There was a sharp pounding at the front door, combined with the doorbell's urgent ringing. Doris, feeling as if she didn't know where to look first, pressed stop on the machine and went to the front door. She opened it and was confused to see Zack Markus standing there looking extremely agitated. "Oh . . . hello," she said. "Kelsey's dad, right?"

"Where are they?"

She blinked in confusion. "I'm sorry?"

"Where are my daughter and your son?" he said accusingly.

Doris's eyes narrowed in annoyance. "I have no idea what you're talking about, but I can tell you this: If you don't calm down, I'm going to slam this door in your face. And if you don't go away, I'm going to call the police."

"I *am* a policeman."

"Really? Can I see your identification?"

Zack hesitated and then admitted, "I'm . . . no longer with the force."

"I see," Doris said. "Let me guess: You lost your temper and were fired."

"No. I was discharged because I was shot in the hip in the line of duty, stopping a liquor store holdup."

"Oh." Doris suddenly felt terrible. "So . . . that's why you . . ."

"Limp, yes." Zack took in a deep breath and let it out slowly. "Look . . . Doris . . . I'm just . . . I'm very worried about Kelsey. And if she's really not here and you don't know what I'm talking about, then we've all got some serious problems. Can I—?"

She stepped away from the door and gestured for him to enter. He did so, trying as hard as he could not to limp at all. He made his way over to a chair and sat. As soon as he did, he reached into his jacket and pulled out a copy of the permission slip he had printed off Kelsey's computer. "Did Josh give you something that looks like this?"

She took it and stared at it. Her newly purchased frozen dinners were thawing on the kitchen table, but she had forgotten about them. "Yes. I signed this yesterday. They were going on a class trip to a museum. . . . No?" she added when she saw him shaking his head.

"Some woman from the school, a Mrs. Faber . . ."

"Farber," corrected Doris, glancing in the direction of the kitchen answering machine.

"Right, her. She called and said there was no school trip." He looked at the permission slip. "According to this, the 'school trip' was going to run late and they weren't going to be back until this evening. So obviously they wanted to be able to go somewhere that was going to keep them away from home until late, and not have us wondering where they were."

"But . . . where did they go? The movies? The mall? Why would they—?"

"Read this."

He pulled out a sheaf of papers, unfolded them carefully, and handed them to Doris. She sat down opposite him and began to read. A few sentences in, she stopped and looked up. "This is from Kelsey's diary," she said uncomfortably. "I'm . . . I'm not sure I should . . . that we should . . ."

"Look . . . Doris . . . you don't know me," he said. "But reading Kelsey's private thoughts isn't something I do routinely. And I wouldn't be doing it now if I weren't worried that she's in deep trouble. The fact is that most of what she's written there is about Josh, and I think you need to see it."

Doris hesitated, then nodded and started reading again. Her eyes got wider and wider the further she went. "I . . . I had no idea," she finally said. "I mean . . . I knew that he loved his comics, and he loved Mascot. But that he identified with a comic book so strongly . . . that he actually thought he and this character were connected somehow . . ." She read aloud from the entry. "'Josh seems so determined to stop the comic from coming out, and he wants my help. He needs me. I've got to do whatever I can, because if I don't, he's just going to go off and do it himself. Telling his mom or my dad won't do any good. They won't believe him and they'll try to stop him, and if there's one thing I've learned about Josh, it's that he's pretty hard to stop. Plus . . . I know it's ridiculous . . . but what if he's right? What if Mascot dies and Josh dies too? How can I live with that?'" She looked up from the diary and said, "Your daughter has quite an imagination."

"She's an amateur compared to your son."

Doris forced a smile. "That's . . . true enough."

"All right. Since they're not here, we have to start making calls." He pulled out his cell phone.

"You're calling the police," Doris said nervously.

He looked up at her. "Of course. We've got two missing children."

"Yes. Of course. I . . . of course."

Zack hesitated, holding his cell phone but not immediately dialing. "What's wrong?"

"Nothing. We . . . we have to call. Naturally. Call them."

Slowly he lowered the phone. "Doris, what are you not telling me?"

"It doesn't matter." She got up, and her hands were

moving in vague, nervous gestures. "The kids are missing, and—"

"*Doris?*"

It all spilled out of Doris then, everything that Mrs. Farber had said and the talk of social services and her worry that they would try to take Josh away from her because she was a terrible mother and she should have done something about this earlier.

By that point Zack was pulling tissues out of the tissue box on the small table next to him and handing them to Doris, whose eyes were stinging with tears. "I'm sorry, I'm sorry," she kept saying. "Please, by all means, call the—"

"That may not be necessary," said Zack as he slid the phone back into his jacket pocket. He pulled himself to a standing position, grunting slightly and trying not to look like he was in pain. "Look . . . this town isn't all that big. I know a few people—I can make a few calls in a nonofficial capacity. . . ."

"Are you sure . . . ?"

"Of course I'm sure." He started to head for the door. "I'll get right on it, and you just—"

He stopped and turned in confusion when he heard a phone being dialed. There was Doris, standing there with the receiver to her ear. "Yes . . . 911 . . . I need to report two missing children . . . yes, I'll hold, but please make it quick. . . ." She put her hand to the speaker and said, "You were going to call as soon as you were out the door, weren't you?"

"Yeah."

"How about we work together and start being honest with each other. Deal?"

"Deal," he said.

CHAPTER 7

DANGER RIDES THE RAILS!

L ooking right and left, Mascot slowly makes his way down the corridor of the lurching train known throughout the world as the Orient Express.

He is doing everything he can to elude those who have been pursuing him and Captain Major. The quest to discover who has framed the Captain and sent them both on the run has led Mascot to this famed train as it lurches along its route between . . . some big city and some other big city in the Orient.

Mascot is doing his best to cope with the fact that Captain Major has disappeared. He knows beyond a doubt that the Captain would never simply abandon him. It is obvious that the evil forces behind this frame job have captured him! And a frame job is what this most definitely is. One of the Captain's most formidable foes has convinced the world that the Captain is actually a fearsome criminal, and now the Captain and Mascot have been trying to stay one step ahead of the authorities while fighting to establish their innocence. Oh, the brilliance of this plan that sets the Captain against his former allies. All those global organizations that used to depend on his help have now turned against him. Mascot has to grudgingly give credit where it's due: Whoever has contrived to come up with this scheme has outdone himself.

But who? Who could it be? The Mad Mannequin? The Lopsider? Mr. Inside Out? Sir Apropos of Nothing? Perhaps the dreaded Silver Dragoness? It could be any or even all of them.

Mascot and the Captain became separated somewhere in the vast . . . um . . . Orient Station. Mascot had already boarded the train and gotten to his seat and then, to his horror, saw the Captain through the window, battling a group of killer ninjas. It was too late: The train was already in motion. And it was an express, so there was no way for him to get off and return to aid his friend and mentor. It's not as if he's worried that Captain Major can't handle himself. In fact, he is convinced that the Captain will somehow manage to get to their destination in the Orient before Mascot even arrives. Still, there's a gnawing uncertainty that is gnawing at him, the way that gnawing uncertainties tend to . . . gnaw.

But Mascot knows he must put these concerns aside and focus instead on the mission at hand. He and Captain Major are supposed to meet with a potential informant on the Orient Express, who will provide them with proof on a microchip that Captain Major has been framed. He doesn't know the informant's name. All he knows is the following: The informant will be dressed in white, and they are to speak a predetermined coded exchange.

Mascot keeps his eyes open, looking for the slightest sign of danger or ambush. He is not clad in his customary costume and mask, but instead is wearing a brilliant disguise that makes him look no different from any other young boy. Still, there's no telling if enemy operatives are on the train, and whether they are capable of penetrating his false guise, no matter how clever he might think it is.

He steps from the fourth car into the fifth. The tracks speed past him below and he vaults from one car to the next effortlessly. This train car is different from the others; it appears to be some sort of lounge car. He scans the crowd and spots his contact. It's a woman, dressed in white, tall and thin. Quite a remarkable individual. She's probably risking life and limb to get this much-needed information to where it can do the most good.

Mascot sidles over and says in a low voice, "The nightingale sings only at daybreak."

She stares at him, her face impassive. "Whatever," she replies.

Perfect. Code phrase given, code response provided. Mascot has to admit that she's quite a cool customer, this one.

"Chip," says Mascot, adopting her terse manner.

She nods, and seconds later Mascot is holding the valuable evidence close to his chest. He makes his way through the train, his heart pounding with growing excitement. This is it: He's holding the proof of Captain Major's innocence. Now all he has to do is find a way to . . .

He senses the danger before he sees it. He has just stepped through to the next car when suddenly his head whips around and he sees the man in black heading right toward him.

A ninja!

Clad head to toe in the sort of dark clothing that enables him to blend with the shadows, the ninja bears down upon Mascot. In the ninja's right hand is a gleaming metal instrument: a sai, the vicious stabbing implement favored by this sort of assassin. The sai gleams in a brief flash of sunlight, and then the ninja is in the car with Mascot.

Mascot glances right and left. The train car is crowded. Too many innocent people who could possibly wind up in the line of fire. This is no place for a battle. Mascot knows he has to keep moving, stay one step ahead of the ninja.

Large Lass. She's Mascot's best bet for ending the battle quickly. With her power to turn things superheavy, she can disable the ninja, no

problem. That way no innocent lives will be put
at risk.

But can he get to her before the ninja gets
to him?

Mascot tosses aside all efforts at subtlety and
takes off at a dead run. The shadow warrior comes
right after him. He is shouting things in his native
ninja tongue. Mascot doesn't understand what he's
saying, but doesn't care. All he knows is that he has
to stay ahead of him long enough to get to Large
Lass.

He charges forward, making it to the next
door, sliding it open as fast as he can, and then
slamming it shut as he dashes into the next car,
nearly colliding with a priest. He mutters a quick
apology and keeps going. Mascot doesn't slow, his
sneakered feet pounding along the floor. He
throws open another door, charges between the
cars. . . .

In his haste he trips. He tumbles forward,
landing on the rickety platform that bridges the
span between the two cars. He clutches like a rabid
bat. The tracks hurtle past below him at blinding
speed. He takes a breath, pulls himself together,

and gets to his feet once more. But he has lost distance, and now the ninja is almost upon him.

The door behind him is still open. He lashes out with his foot and kicks the protruding handle just as the ninja is reaching for him. The door slams shut, the ninja barely yanking his hand out of the way in time. Mascot wastes no time, bounding to his feet and running into the next car.

Large Lass is seated, waiting for him. Next to her is her faithful sidekick, Waistline. They look up at him curiously, unaware that danger is mere steps behind.

Before Mascot can get a word out, the ninja has come up behind him and grabbed him by the arm. He whips Mascot around. Mascot draws back his power punch, ready to take a stand. Why isn't Large Lass activating her mass powers? What sort of ally is she, anyway? Maybe she—

"What the heck is your problem?"

—doesn't realize the magnitude of the threat. She believes this to be Mascot's fight and is loath to violate the superhero code by horning in on—

"You could have broken my hand!"

"He's sorry, sir," Kelsey said quickly. "Aren't you sorry, Josh? Tell the conductor you're sorry."

"Sorry," muttered Josh.

The conductor, a young Asian man, stared at Josh for a long moment before finally releasing him. He made no attempt to hide just how annoyed he was. He was holding a ticket puncher in one hand. In the other hand was a fist-ful of singles. "I was just trying to give you your change. You left it back at the snack bar. And you start running from me, like . . . like I don't know what."

"I was worried you might be a ninja."

Kelsey rolled her eyes and—maybe a bit too dramati-cally—slapped her forehead with her hand. Paul just stared. So did the conductor. "A ninja?" he finally echoed.

Shaking his head, the conductor handed Josh the money. Josh took it with his free hand, the other hand clutching the bag of chips that he'd gone to buy for Kelsey.

"A ninja," said the conductor once more, and then he looked suspiciously at the threesome. "Where are your parents?"

"Home," said Josh.

He tilted his head toward Paul. "Who's this?"

"My big brother," Kelsey said immediately. Paul, to Josh's

astonishment, didn't react at all. He didn't seem surprised that Kelsey had just identified him as an older sibling. Instead he just smiled vaguely in the conductor's direction.

"This is a train, not a playground," said the conductor.

"Okay," Paul said.

The conductor nodded once more, as if assuring himself that he'd handled the situation, and then walked away muttering to himself, "A ninja. Unbelievable."

Sheepishly, Josh handed the chips to Kelsey. She leaned in toward him and said in a sharp whisper, "Are you *trying* to get us in trouble?"

"I just . . ."

"You just what?"

Mascot knows that they cannot be too careful. Enemies lurk everywhere, and although this "conductor" person was harmless . . . the way of the ninja is crafty.

He shrugged again. "I dunno."

"You dunno. Sheesh." Kelsey ripped open the bag of chips. The chips flew everywhere, and she moaned. "See what you made me do?"

Josh, who was sitting across from her, didn't quite

understand how he was responsible, but he wisely chose not to defend himself.

Paul abruptly looked at Kelsey and asked, "Am I really your big brother?"

In the midst of gathering up the scattered chips, Kelsey froze. She looked up at Paul. "Well . . . uh . . . no."

"Then why did you tell him I was?"

Kelsey looked at Josh for help, but he didn't have much more of a clue what to say than Kelsey did.

"Are you guys running away?" said Paul.

"What? No! No, we're not—" Kelsey's voice was louder than she would have liked, and she brought it down quickly. "We're not running away."

"Do your mom and dad know where you are?"

"She doesn't have a mom, and my dad . . . isn't around," Josh told him.

"Oh." Paul looked saddened by that. "I don't have a mom or a dad either."

Kelsey and Josh exchanged looks. It had been difficult enough for them, coping with only having one parent. The notion of having none—that was too much.

"Who took care of you?" said Josh, who really was more interested in what had happened to Paul's parents but couldn't quite bring himself to ask.

"Mostly my uncle, but all kinds of people," said Paul, looking into the distance. "There have always been different people taking care of me. But now," he said with a touch of pride, "I take care of myself. And I guess," he added almost as an afterthought, "I could take care of you guys."

"Sure," said Josh and Kelsey at almost the same time.

"That'd be nice. I never had people to take care of before. I took care of some goldfish once. And a cat."

"Well, it's not that much different, taking care of people," said Josh.

"The cat ate all the goldfish and then got sick and died."

"Oh," said Josh.

"I see," said Kelsey.

The train continued to speed on its way toward Northchester.

CHAPTER 8

MOM AND DAD HIT THE ROAD

The ticket seller only had to look at the picture Zack Markus showed him for a couple of seconds, and then he nodded and handed it back. Speaking from the other side of a thick glass window, he grinned and said, "Yup. I remember her. Came by early this morning, bought two bus tickets—for herself and the young man who was with her. Kid brother, I figured."

"It never occurred to you," Zack said very slowly, "that maybe selling two bus tickets to a couple of kids wasn't the brightest idea?"

"Kids?" The ticket seller looked surprised. "The girl looked to be . . . what? Sixteen? Seventeen?"

Zack shook his head. "She's thirteen."

"*Thirteen?*" He was astounded. "She looked much older. Acted like it, too. Very self-assured young lady."

"Yeah, well . . . she gets it from her mother."

The ticket seller finally got it. "You're her dad. I mean, you flashed your badge and everything, so I knew you were a cop . . . but you're her dad."

Zack knew that he really shouldn't be showing his badge around and acting as if he were still on duty. He typically didn't even carry it with him. The work he did at the police station was strictly on a volunteer basis—something to do so he wouldn't go completely crazy. But he'd stopped at home and gotten it before heading out to investigate Kelsey's disappearance. It was a way to get things done, especially in a town that didn't have a lot of police officers.

"Yeah. That's right. I'm her dad."

"You should be very proud. That's quite a young lady you're raising."

"Thanks," said Zack impatiently. "Where were they going?"

"New York City. Port Authority."

He hesitated and then asked, "Round-trip tickets?"

"Of course!" The ticket seller started to laugh, and then he saw the expression on Zack's face and the laughter faded. "Of course," he said, much more seriously. "Look, officer, I wouldn't worry about those kids. The boy seemed a little twitchy, but the girl, she's got a solid head on her shoulders. Kids today, it's not like when you and I were little. They can pretty much handle anything. They probably just went into the city to see some sights. They'll be back before you know it. . . ."

"Would you be saying that if one of your kids took off to New York City?"

The ticket seller's gaze fell. "Probably not. I'd probably be out of my mind worrying."

"Welcome to my world," said Zack.

The squad car that had been parked outside the Miller house was still there when Zack returned, and he brought both Doris and Officer Daniel Wiener up to speed about what he'd learned.

"If you're certain they're up there," offered Wiener, "we can alert the New York police."

Zack smiled bitterly. "It's New York City, Danny. On any given day they're investigating thousands of serious crimes. Two kids who weren't abducted and have been missing for less than a day . . . that's not even going to get on their radar. I'm going to handle this."

"I'm coming too," said Doris.

"What if they come back here?"

"I'll call my neighbor. She'll come over and house-sit. If the kids come home, she'll call me and we turn right around."

"Forget it."

Doris stared at him and then said, "Okay, okay, fine. I'll stay. But call the publishing office first. See if they're there."

"Yeah. Yeah, that's a good idea."

Doris headed into the kitchen while Zack pulled out his cell phone, dialed information for the number, and quickly called Wonder Comics. He found himself thwarted, however, by the company's voice mail system. He was unable to get a human being on the phone. He couldn't use the automated company directory because he had no idea who to ask for, and his attempts to dial the operator got him nowhere. "How does the operator have voice mail? Where's the sense in that?" he demanded. Wiener just shrugged.

"This is ridiculous," said Zack. "I can be in Manhattan in less than an hour. Danny, you can head back to the station.

No use your hanging around here."

"What about Mrs. Miller?' asked Wiener.

"Tell her to wish me luck."

Zack limped toward his convertible parked in the driveway and stopped dead a few feet away.

Doris was sitting in the passenger seat. She looked up at him blandly. "Hey there."

Zack was about to argue and then gave up, saying only, "Just . . . don't start telling me what to do, okay?"

"You're in charge."

He pulled the car out, did a U-turn, and headed down the street.

"How are you planning to drive to Manhattan?" she asked.

"Turnpike to the Holland Tunnel."

"Take the Lincoln Tunnel. It's faster."

Zack groaned.

Terry Fogarty was Doris's next-door neighbor. A middle-aged woman whose hair seemed to be perpetually in curlers, she was sitting in the living room as per Doris's request, waiting and hoping and praying that the kids would come home safe and sound and all this craziness would be over. So when the doorbell rang, she sprang from the easy chair and ran over as quickly as her stubby legs would allow. She was disappointed when she opened the door to discover that the kids were not, in fact, there. Instead there was a woman with a pinched expression, and standing behind her was another woman, taller, with dark hair and stooping shoulders. "I'm sorry, we're not interested in buying anything," said Mrs. Fogarty.

"We're not selling anything," said the taller woman, and she held up official-looking identification. "I'm Ellen Sanchez from social services. Mrs. Farber," and she indicated the woman standing next to her, "has informed me that there's a dangerous situation going on here. I'd like to speak to Mrs. Miller, please."

"Well . . . she's not here at the moment," said Terry.

Mrs. Farber's mouth twisted into a nasty smile. "Let me guess: She's out trying to find her runaway son."

Terry knew this was exactly the case, but she wasn't about to admit it to this very unpleasant-looking woman. So she just shrugged and said, "I couldn't say."

"Couldn't? Or wouldn't?" demanded Mrs. Sanchez. When Mrs. Fogarty didn't reply immediately, she continued, "We'd like to come in and wait for her, if you don't mind."

"As a matter of fact, I think I do," Terry told them. "I'm

leaning toward slamming the door in your face."

"Ma'am," said Mrs. Sanchez, keeping her voice polite, but there was a cut of iron to it. "You can do that if you want. And then I can go back and get a court order insisting that we be given entrance so we can inspect the premises. And then you'll have no choice."

"Well then," Terry said pleasantly, "I guess that's what you'll have to do, isn't it? Good day." With that, she closed the door. Then she leaned with her back against the door and let out a low, long whistle. "Ohhhh, Doris," she moaned, "what has your son gotten you into?"

Michael Galton was the president and publisher of Wonder Comics, and he was none too happy.

A comics veteran of some forty years' standing, he was built kind of like an egg; he even tended to rock back and forth in his chair as if he were perched on a wall and about to tip over at any time. His mostly bald head added to his general eggish appearance.

His office was filled with assorted toys, books, and games based on Wonder Comics characters. It was also filled with people at the moment: a Mrs. Miller and Mr. Markus, who were worried about their kids; Florence, the receptionist; and Joe from down in the mailroom—

all talking over one another.

"So let me get this straight. The kids hooked up with this Paul person and convinced him to take them to Kirby," said Mr. Markus. He talked with a clipped manner, biting off the ends of his words. He sounded like a television policeman.

"But how could they do that?" said Mrs. Miller. "I mean, what sort of adult would let himself be talked into something like that by a couple of kids?"

"Yeah, well," said Joe, shifting uncomfortably in his chair, "Paul isn't what you'd call a typical adult."

"What . . . does that mean?" asked Mr. Markus.

Galton stepped in. "Paul is . . . well, he's . . . very trusting. And very eager to lend a hand. And very dependable. So if your kids said that they needed help, then his instinct is going to be to help them. Look, the fact is, he's my nephew, and I've known him since he was a kid. If your children are with Paul, then they're in good hands."

"That may be," said Mr. Markus. "But what we need to do—what *you* need to do . . . is pick up the phone and call this Stan Kirby fellow."

"He doesn't own a telephone."

"He doesn't . . . ?" Mr. Markus's voice trailed off. Then he recovered and said, "It's the twenty-first century. Who in the world doesn't own a telephone?"

"Someone who doesn't want to hear from people," said Galton. "Mr. Markus"—he leaned forward, resting his hands on his desk and interlacing his fingers—"I co-founded this company with Stan Kirby over thirty years ago. I can only tell you that, as far back as I can remember, Stan's been his own man. He doesn't do what everyone else expects him to do. At the height of this company's popularity, he asked me to buy out his ownership so he could just sit in a studio and write and draw comics. And he doesn't have a phone. He *does* own a computer. I think he even goes online sometimes. But he doesn't read email for weeks at a time."

"Then we've got no way of getting in touch with him. No way to tell him to keep my daughter and Mrs. Miller's son there."

"No, but I can do the next best thing." He tapped the intercom button. "Sheila? Get me Tom Harrelson, would you?" Anticipating their question, he said, "He's the sheriff in Northchester, where Stan lives now."

"How do you know the sheriff up in Northchester?"

Galton grinned. "He was a letter hack."

"A what?"

"Letter hack. Used to write letters to our comics all the

time. Tommy Harrelson. Had a great eye for detail, ton of imagination. Kept running into him at conventions through the years. That's the great thing about being in this business a long time: You actually see some of the fans grow up and make something of themselves. Believe me, if anyone can understand the way your boy thinks and can round him up for us, it's Sheriff Harrelson. In fact, when Stan was looking to move out of Manhattan, to get away from the rat race here, I was the one who talked him into going up to Northchester because I knew Tom was there and would keep an eye on him."

Galton's intercom buzzed at him. "I've got Sheriff Harrelson for you."

"Thanks, Sheila." Galton punched the speakerphone button and said cheerily, "Tom. Mike Galton here. How's it going?"

"Not too well, Mike, truth to tell," Harrelson's voice returned.

"Why, what's wrong?"

"You guys are killing Mascot? How can you kill Mascot? He's a brilliant character."

Zack Markus looked at Mrs. Miller with open incredulity.

"I sympathize with you, Tom. But that's how the readers

voted. Not much we can do about it. Anyway, that's not why I'm calling you. We've got a bit of a problem, and we're kind of hoping you and your boys can pitch in before things get a lot worse."

CHAPTER 9

THINGS GET A LOT WORSE

"Are you being Mascot now?" Large Lass asks him with a skeptical eye. "Or are you being Josh? I really need to know."

Mascot hesitates a moment.

"I'm Josh, Kelsey. Who else would I be?" says Mascot.

"I, just . . . I wasn't sure," Large Lass tells him. "When you're being all Mascot-y, you get this kind of look in your eye and your voice gets a little *deeper, and that's how you're talking now."*

"I'm talking this way because there's people all around us and I'm just trying to keep my voice down," Mascot explains, sounding convincing even to himself. Then he pauses and says, "Y'know . . . most girls would find Mascot a lot more exciting than plain old Josh Miller."

"Yeah, well . . . I'm not most girls."

Having no idea how to respond to that—and frankly disconcerted over the notion that Large Lass would find plain old Josh more exciting than a costumed identity because that's just not how it's supposed to work—Mascot glances around the train, making sure that there are no more ninjas hiding in the shadows, waiting to spring out at them. "Okay, fine. So anyway . . . here's the thing: We have to remember that people are going to be trying to stop us."

"What people?" asks Waistline nervously.

"Any people. They could come at us at any time, from any direction. And especially we have to watch out for the police. They're out to get us."

"How do you know?"

<u>*Because they're convinced that Captain Major and*</u>

I are criminals! Haven't you been paying attention?

Mascot realizes before the words come out that if he says that, it's going to make Large Lass realize that she is, in fact, talking to Mascot, rather than to Josh. He realizes that the only thing he can do is turn back into Josh.

"Because that's what happens in the comic," Josh told her.

"Right. Right. I keep forgetting that."

"What, you don't believe me after all this?"

"After all what?" said Kelsey. "Look, Josh . . ." She tried to smile, but it didn't come easily. "I've just been trying to help you. You know that. I want you to be happy, and it . . . look, it just hurt to see you so upset. I'm just . . . I'm getting worried, that's all. I figured we'd come to the city, see Stan Kirby, and . . ."

"And what?"

"And that maybe he'd talk to you and make you feel better about all this or make you at least realize that it's all just coincidence. That the things that happen in the comic aren't going to happen to you in real life."

"I'm not sure I have a real life anymore," Josh told her.

"The point is, I didn't know everything was going

to get this involved."

"If you had," he said, "would you still have come?"

Kelsey tried to imagine letting Josh go off by himself on this crazy adventure, and she just couldn't do it. "Probably," she admitted.

"Good," he said. "So look . . . when the police come after us—"

"The police aren't going to come after us!" said Kelsey, feeling exasperated with him all over again. "Your mom and my dad think we're off on a school trip! We haven't broken any laws!"

"But they're coming after Mascot in the comic!" Paul blurted out.

"Exactly!" Josh said triumphantly.

Annoyed, Kelsey looked at Paul. "You're just encouraging him."

Paul in turn looked to Josh, who sighed with the air of the truly put-upon. "She doesn't get it yet. But she will. She just has to see it for herself."

"Northchester!"

It was the conductor, walking down the aisle, calling out, "Northchester! Last stop! All passengers must disembark at Northchester!" He glanced at Josh before he passed by, clearly pleased that the pesky boy would be getting off his train.

"So how do we get from here to Mr. Kirby?" Kelsey asked Paul.

"Oh, there's a bus that goes right from the train station and drops me off a block or so from his house. So I figure that's what we'll take."

They nodded, and as the train rolled into the station, Paul and Kelsey got out of their seats. Josh, however, remained frozen, looking out the window. His eyes were wide and his face turned slightly pale. When Josh didn't follow them, Kelsey turned back. "What's wrong?" she said, and then leaned in to see what it was he was watching.

The train platform opened out into a parking lot, and situated smack in the middle was a police car. A uniformed officer was standing there. He was holding a sheet of paper in either hand and studying the train, glancing from the paper to the train.

To Kelsey's surprise, Josh pulled a small pair of binoculars from his pants pocket. "Where'd you get those from?" she asked.

Mascot smiles inwardly. How can Large Lass be unaware of Mascot's famed utility pockets, which provide him with whatever tool he needs to handle any situation?

Josh didn't bother to answer. Instead he used them to focus on the paper that the police officer was holding. The train was coming in from a side angle, so he had a clear view of it. "It's a picture of you," he said, "and a picture of me."

"How . . . how did he . . . ?"

"It's in the comic. There's a scene where the police are searching for Mascot and they have a picture of him." He stared at her. "Do you believe me now?"

"I . . ." She shook her head, trying to wrap her mind around it. "Maybe . . . maybe my dad figured out we were gone. Maybe he faxed pictures to—"

"To *Northchester*?" Josh said skeptically. "Come on."

"So, what, your answer is that they're chasing you because they're chasing Mascot in the comic?"

"Hey, of the two of us, which one said that this was going to happen, huh?"

Kelsey didn't have an answer for that.

Paul, however, was looking extremely nervous. "Am . . . am I going to get into trouble? On TV, the police come for you because you did something wrong. Did I do something wrong? I don't want to go to jail."

"You're not going to go to jail," Josh told him with certainty. "None of us are. I'm not going down like this. Not without a fight."

"You're not going to *fight* a *policeman*!" said Kelsey.

Josh didn't answer. Instead he darted across the aisle and peered out the window on the opposite side. "Okay. There's some kind of forest or woods preserve or something on the other side. If we can get to that without him seeing us, we lose him. We're in the last car. All you have to do is go out, circle around back of the train, and get to the woods."

"What about you?"

"I'm going to distract him so he doesn't see you guys going."

"How?"

Ninja training.

"Just get to the end of this car and get ready for the distraction."

"How will we know what the distraction is?"

"Trust me."

Josh jumped off the seat, headed into the bathroom,

and closed the door. Paul and Kelsey exchanged confused looks. "I guess he really had to go!" Paul said.

Once in the bathroom, Josh carefully stood on the edge of the toilet, reached up, grabbed the latches on the window, and slid it down. It was a half window, designed to slide only a short way. But it was all Josh needed. Carefully he slid his thin body through the opening far too narrow for either Kelsey or Paul, but just wide enough for—

—Mascot. As he contorts his body to get through the opening, he looks right and left and sees the other track below him. Fortunately there is no train coming from the other direction or he'd be in deep trouble. Also fortunately, the bathroom is on the opposite side of the train from the parking lot. He could easily escape into the woods, leaving Large Lass and Waistline behind. But he cannot bring himself to do that . . . and besides, Waistline is the only one who knows how to get to their destination.

He takes a deep breath, swings his legs up and through, and moments later drops to the ground on the far side of the train. Now . . . now comes the trickiest and most hazardous part. "Kids," he mutters, "under no circumstance should you try this at home. It should be left only to the professional superheroes and their sidekicks."

He runs to the front end of the train, staying low, and then—knowing that the policeman is watching people emerging through the doors—he crawls down under the train. <u>Don't let it start moving, don't let it start moving,</u> he thinks as he clambers underneath. He's grateful that this type of train doesn't ride on an electrified third rail, but instead an overhead electrical cable, or else he'd be upping the danger quotient even more.

Crawling on his belly, Mascot scrapes up his shirt as he emerges unseen on the other side. He waits to make certain that nobody is looking in his direction, then scrambles out from underneath. He lets out a low "Whewwwww" and takes refuge behind a large trash can. The police officer has now walked away from his police car, and he's showing the picture to people getting off the train. They're shaking their heads or shrugging. But it's only a matter of time before the cop finds someone who has seen them . . . such as the ninja disguised as a train conductor. Mascot knew they were in cahoots.

Seizing his opportunity, Mascot sprints toward

the cop car. He has to move as fast as he can, employing all the stealth technique and ninja skill that Captain Major taught him. He gets to the police car and opens the passenger side door. His plan is to start the car up and send it rolling forward so that the cop will have to chase after it. But there are two problems: The cop didn't leave the keys in the car, and Mascot suddenly remembers he doesn't know how to drive. Perhaps, he reasons, he can find some sort of emergency button to push that will simply start the car up. Leaning forward, he begins pushing dials and buttons at random.

An ear-splitting howl rips from the police car. The siren. Mascot has activated the siren.

Okay. That works.

He darts away from the police car, staying low, using other parked cars to shield him from sight as he sees the annoyed police officer heading back to his unit. Mascot keeps moving and gets to the back end of the train just in time to see Large Lass and Waistline scrambling out the door. They give each other a thumbs-up, and Large Lass looks impressed by his ingenuity.

"Come on!" he says. He knows they won't have

long. The three of them dart around the end of the train, come around the other side, scamper across the empty tracks, and head for the woods . . .

. . . and stop dead.

There is a mesh fence, about six feet high, right up against the forest that runs the length of the platform. Mascot hadn't realized it was there because of the shadows of the overhanging trees.

They stand on the very edge of the tracks and study the situation.

"Okay. No problem. We just climb it," says Mascot.

"Sure," says Waistline.

Large Lass stares at them as if they have both lost their minds. "You think I'm climbing this?" she demands.

"Why not?"

"I'm not exactly built for climbing, y'know."

"It'll be fine. We'll help you."

Mascot runs up to the fence, grabs it, and starts climbing. It takes him no time at all. "Now you help her over," says Mascot to Waistline.

But Waistline is staring off into the distance. "Uh-oh," he says softly.

"What . . . ?"

Mascot looks to see what Waistline is looking at, as does Large Lass.

There's a train coming.

They're standing right at the edge of the track. They're not going to be clear of it. It's in the distance, but it's moving fast.

The train that they arrived on is still sitting at the station on the other track. If Large Lass and Waistline pull away from the fence and try to run back around the train, they might not make it in time. Even if they did, the police officer would then see them for sure.

It's the fence or nothing.

"Hurry!" says Mascot urgently.

Large Lass desperately plants her feet between the links in the fence and tries to pull herself up. She grunts, frustrated, frightened, casting frequent glances in the train's direction. "Stop looking at it!" shouts Mascot.

Waistline is behind her and tries to help. He grunts under her weight as he pushes and prods and shoves as hard as he can. Large Lass is now halfway up the fence, and the oncoming train has covered

half the distance between itself and the runaway
heroes. The train blasts its horn. There's no way it's
going to be able to stop in time.

It pounds toward them like a great metal
monster as Large Lass's stomach thuds against the
top part of the fence. "I can't do it! I can't get
over!" she shouts.

"Yes you can!" Mascot tells her. "Use your
powers!"

"What?"

"Make yourself superlight!"

<u>"I'm supposed to start dieting now?!?"</u>

Waistline continues to push. Large Lass tries to
boost herself over. Her foot slips. She sags back
down, losing height, and now the train is almost
upon them. The horn is screeching at them. Mascot
can just barely glimpse the alarmed expression of
the engineer as he sees they're not going to be able
to get clear in time. Mascot clambers back up onto
the fence, grabs Large Lass's wrists, and pulls as
hard as he can to try to get her over. Even if they
manage it, it seems impossible that Waistline is
going to have time to clear it as well.

The train is horrifically close.

Large Lass screams.

The fence collapses beneath them.

Not the entire fence: just the section that they're on. Unable to bear up under the combined force of Waistline's shoving, Mascot's pulling, and Large Lass's weight, the portion of the fence crumbles toward Mascot. Large Lass collapses right on top of him while Waistline is pitched forward, tumbling to the side. The train roars past seconds later, the ground shaking beneath them.

Mascot lies there for a moment and then, once the train has passed and he can hear himself think, he says, "Superheavy works too."

"We could have been killed!" Kelsey shouted as she scrambled off him. "Don't you get that? We could have been killed! Do you have any idea what that's like, knowing that?"

"Of course I do!" Josh shouted right back at her, getting to his feet. "Now you know how I feel!"

He stood there for a moment, seething, his fingers curled into fists, and then he turned and stomped away. He walked about twenty feet into the woods and then stopped and leaned against a tree, his back to them.

Paul scratched his head and shifted from one foot to the other uncomfortably. "What should we do?"

Kelsey looked at him. It felt weird to her, having an adult asking her what should be done. She was used to adults telling her what to do . . . teachers in general and her father in particular. Kelly knew that Paul wasn't like other adults . . . that he was closer to her in his thought processes than he was to her dad. Still . . . it was just . . . odd.

Seeing that he was waiting for an answer, she told him, "Wait here." She strode over to Josh. She didn't actually have the slightest idea what she was going to say to him, but she figured that whatever it was, she should sound certain about it.

She stepped over several fallen branches—and almost lost her footing and fell into some brush—before she finally got to where Josh was standing. "Josh," she began, not knowing what the next words she was going to speak were.

She didn't have the opportunity.

Usually when Josh spoke, even in normal conversation . . . or at least as close to "normal" as conversation with Josh ever was . . . it was from somewhere deep in his chest as if he were on a stage and trying to project his voice to audience members in the balcony. He made big gestures and spoke in broad and sweeping statements. In short, he acted as he imagined a superhero should act, or at least that was Kelsey's interpretation of it.

He wasn't acting that way now. His shoulders were slumped and his voice was tinged with something alien to him: defeat. He spoke so softly that at first she didn't hear him, and when she asked him to repeat himself and he obliged, it was hard for her to believe that this was actually Josh talking.

"I think"—he raised his voice slightly so she could hear him properly—"maybe you should go home."

"What?" That was what she had said the first time, but at that point it was because she genuinely couldn't hear him. Now it was from surprise.

"I said," and for him it was the third time but he didn't act annoyed that he was being made to repeat himself over and over again, "maybe you should go home."

"Without you?"

He shrugged.

"Josh, what are you talking about? Why should I . . . ?"

He peered over at her, and to her astonishment she saw that his eyes were wet with tears. He wiped his arm across them hurriedly. "You were almost killed."

"*I* told *you* that."

"Yeah, and I'm agreeing with you." He looked miserable. "It was my fault. This whole thing is my fault. Me a culprit, me a maximum culprit."

She blinked in confusion. "What does *that* mean?"

"I dunno. It's something my father would say when Mom was arguing with him and telling him everything that was wrong with him. *Culprit* means bad guy. I know that from the comics. So I guess it means that I'm the bad guy."

"You're not a bad guy, Josh. It's just . . ."

He wasn't listening to her. Instead he got to his feet and said, "Look . . . the policeman is probably still out there. You go to him, you tell him you want him to take you home. If something happened to you, it would be all my fault, and I just . . . I can't deal with that. I can't. Okay?"

He started to walk away, and she grabbed him by the arm and spun him around. He looked surprised when she did so, startled by her strength. "First of all, dummy, you still don't know the address where you're going. Remember?"

"Fine. Paul," he called, "what's Mr. Kirby's address?"

Paul shook his head firmly. "I can't tell you that. You know I'm not allowed to give out addresses."

"But you said you were going to take us to him!"

"I am."

"Then we'll know!"

"Yeah," Paul said in a pleased voice, as if he had managed to work out a really tough problem all by himself, "but taking you isn't the same as telling you. So it's okay."

Josh had no idea what to say to that . . . and his expression was so confused that it was all Kelsey could do not to laugh, despite the seriousness of the situation.

"That's crazy!" Josh finally exclaimed.

"I don't think the kid who's worried that a comic book character dying means he's going to die, too, gets to say that anybody else is crazy," Kelsey pointed out.

"Okay, fine," said Josh. "You know what? I'll . . . I'll find it myself, that's all. I'll ask around. I'll investigate. I'll figure it out. This isn't your problem anyway, Kelsey. It's mine."

"Look . . . here's the thing. . . ."

"There's a thing?"

"It's just . . ." Kelsey took a deep breath and let it out slowly. "I . . . I never thought about dying before. I mean, yeah, my mom died . . . and I know that kids can die . . . but I never thought about it happening to me because, y'know, mostly it happens to grown-ups. And then I saw that train coming at me, and I thought, 'Oh my God, I'm going to die,' and I didn't because, y'know, obviously, I'm right here, but I think I'm always going to remember how I felt at that moment."

"Okay," Josh said slowly. "So . . . ?"

"So . . . maybe I kind of get how it must be for you, that's all. Being afraid you're going to die and everything. I mean . . . I still think it's kind of silly, but it's not silly to you, and if you're scared . . ."

Fear? Silly girl! Mascot doesn't know the meaning of the word <u>fear</u>.

"I'm not scared," he told her confidently. "I'm not scared, because I'm going to stop it. I'm going to save Mascot and save myself, because I'm one of the good guys, and the good guys always win."

"Aren't the police good guys?" Paul asked.

"Yeah."

"Well, that policeman was trying to find you, and he failed, so does that mean he wasn't really a good guy? Or if he was a good guy, then are you the bad guy, which means that sometimes bad guys do win, and if that's the case, then maybe Mascot is going to die?"

Josh stared at Paul for a long moment, and then said,

"Paul, maybe we should get moving?"

"Okeydokey," Paul said cheerfully, and he led them through the woods without having the slightest idea of which way he was going.

CHAPTER 10

ATTACK OF THE MERCS

"**M**ercs? What are mercs?"

Kelsey wasn't remotely familiar with the term. As she stepped carefully through the forest, trying to keep up with Paul's longer strides and Josh's more urgent speed, she said again, "Josh? What are mercs? Why do we have to watch out for them?"

He stopped, waiting for her to catch up. "Because," he said, lowering his voice to a whisper, "the forest is where they always are. Captain Major and Mascot once had to fight a whole squad of them single-handedly."

"What, and that hasn't happened to you yet? How'd you miss that one?" she asked, sounding sarcastic.

"I don't know," he replied in all seriousness. "That's why I'm worried that this is the perfect time and place for it."

"But what are they? Some kind of monsters or something?"

"*Merc* is short for *mercenary*. Guys who are paid soldiers who go anywhere that people will send them if they've got enough money for it."

Kelsey considered it. "If it's short for *mercenary*, then how come the word isn't *merses*? Why is it a *k* sound instead of an *s* sound? It's not *merkenary*."

"I dunno. It just is."

"Nothing 'just is,' Josh," Kelsey said. She was feeling a little out of breath, and she paused, leaning against a tree. "There are reasons for everything when it comes to words."

"Oh yeah?" he said challengingly. "Then if stories are *biblical*, how come they're not stories from the Bibble? *Biblical* is said like there's two *b*'s in it, but it's spelled with one? Is it two *b*'s, or not two *b*'s?"

"That is the question," said Kelsey, and then she laughed.

Josh just shook his head and turned away muttering, "Girls."

"Okay, okay, fine," she said, moving after him again. "That's a fair point, I guess. But I still think that—"

"*Shhhh!*"

Mascot ducks behind a tree, his back against it, and he yanks Large Lass over so that she's right up against him. They're both blocked from view behind the tree, although Mascot is feeling a little uncomfortable about the closeness of their position. Waistline is standing several feet away, looking confused, and Mascot quickly gestures for him to take refuge behind some brush. Waistline does so, practically diving behind it, his backpack bouncing around on his back. "Ow!" he cries out, scratching himself on the very overgrowth that he is trying to hide behind.

Then another voice comes from farther away in the woods. "There! I think they're over there!" It's a low, harsh whisper, an adult voice.

Large Lass's eyes widen in shock. She's not speaking because Mascot has clamped his hand over her mouth to make sure she doesn't utter a word.

She'd been angry with him for doing so at first, but now—with danger imminent—she has bigger things on her mind.

"Quiet! Quiet!" comes another voice, and then a third saying, "You're making more noise telling him to be quiet than anything he was doing," and then the first voice says, "All of you, just shut up! I think it's from over there!" Since Mascot can't see them, naturally he cannot determine where the "over there" that they're referring to is. He has an uncomfortable feeling that he's the "over there" they're looking for.

There is a faint rustling from about a hundred feet away. Then Mascot sees the first of them. He is about medium build, dressed entirely in army camouflage. He is wearing a black stocking mask over his head that obscures his face. Worst of all, he is carrying a pistol, clearly looking for a target. Slowly two more armed men dressed in similar outfits emerge from hiding behind him.

"Mercs," Mascot says under his breath.

Large Lass risks a glance around the tree and gasps. "I don't believe it," she manages to say, as she looks at Mascot in wonder.

"Tol'ja." He shouldn't be boasting; it's beneath him. Still, as much as he'd like to, he can't resist the opportunity. "You should start believing me more."

"Maybe you're right"—and there is something in her voice that Mascot finds very satisfying. She sounds impressed. Well . . . good. Mascot is pretty darned impressive.

"They're coming this way!" Waistline whispers in alarm. "What do we do?"

"We have to take 'em," says Mascot. He looks around and then up. "Give me a boost," he instructs Waistline, lifting his hands in the air.

Waistline does as instructed, gripping Mascot by the hips and then hoisting him up, all the time taking care to stay hidden behind the tree. Mascot reaches upward, fingers grasping, and snags one of the lower-hanging branches. Seconds later he is clambering up into the tree.

Unfortunately he makes some noise as he does so. The tree branches rustle, and this attracts the attention of the mercs. The lead one points in their general direction and says, "There! Over there!"

Immediately they hit the ground, dropping to

their bellies, to present lesser targets. They're smart, these mercs, and clearly battle trained. Mascot, however, has the high ground. That has to count.

The mercs elbow crawl toward them. Mascot desperately wishes he had a weapon of some kind. Then he looks up and his eyes widen.

Sitting there, big as life, and about two feet away from him, is a hornets' nest. There's no sign of movement, but Mascot still recognizes it. Perfect. Absolutely perfect.

Crouched on the long limb, he sees a branch that looks breakable. It's about two feet away from him. Slowly, carefully, hoping that the leaves continue to hide him from view, he crab walks along the limb until he's within reach of the branch. He wraps his fingers around it even as he sees that the mercs are drawing way too close. Large Lass and Waistline are looking up at him, fear in their eyes. No need. He's got everything under control.

He snaps off the branch.

But it makes way too loud a sound.

The mercs look up. "Up there! One of them's up there!" shouts the lead merc, and they bring their weapons up.

Moving as fast as he can, Mascot swings the branch up and over and hits the hornets' nest as hard as he can. He has one shot at it, and he lucks out. The hornets' nest tumbles from overhead, spinning through the air like a soccer ball, and lands squarely in front of the mercs.

They see what it is and immediately yell in alarm. Two of them roll backward, while the third scrambles to his feet and charges forward. Mascot waits for the furious hornets to emerge from the nest in a furious dark cloud of anger that will furiously sting the Mercs with furious . . . uh . . . furiocity.

Nothing. No hornets.

It's a dead nest; the hornets abandoned it who knows how long ago.

The other two mercs haven't realized it yet, but the one closest to the tree does. "Hey!" he says, seeing the lack of insect activity. "It's just a—"

Mascot has no time to consider his next course of action. He just does it. He leaps from the tree, dropping like a rock and landing on the back of the closest merc. The merc staggers but doesn't go down. Mascot, hanging on desperately, grabs at the *merc's mask. He twists it around, and the eyeholes of the mask are yanked to the side. The merc is shouting, "I can't see! Leggo!" He drops his gun. It clatters off a rock and tumbles to one side.*

"It's a kid! It's some kid!" one of the other mercs is yelling, and now all the mercs are on their feet and running toward them.

They're almost there when Waistline steps out into view and roars, "You get out of here!" He is holding a rock, and he throws it as hard as he can. It lands squarely on the chest of one of the mercs, knocking him off his feet.

The merc whom Mascot is clutching grabs around and snags Mascot by the ankle. The merc tries to yank him off, stumbles, and falls. He twists at the last second and lands so that he comes down on top of Mascot. The air is expelled from Mascot's lungs with a loud <u>whuffff!</u> He lies there stunned for a moment. The merc, standing, is twisting his mask around so that he can see again.

That's when they hear a low, frightening growl, a noise that isn't coming from any human throat.

Mascot turns and then freezes.

A monstrous dog is standing about ten feet

away, crouched low to the ground and snarling. It has no collar, no dog tags. Its fur is brown and black. Its body is tense. Its lips are drawn back and its fangs are exposed. The growling, deep in its throat, continues. Foam is welling up from the edges of its mouth. It's probably rabid.

The mercs, all of whom are standing now, see it. As one, they back up slowly.

The growl transforms into a vicious bark and the dog charges.

The mercs scream like little girls and bolt through the woods.

One of them, the one that Mascot had been wrestling with, trips over the fallen hornet's nest. His foot tangling in it, he goes down, sprawling. He cries out for his friends. They keep running.

The terrifying animal starts to pursue them, but then sees the fallen merc and turns toward the easier prey. The merc is terrified. "Get away . . . get away . . . help! Help me! Somebody help me!"

Mascot stands there for a moment, torn. This is a merc. He was out to get them. But now he is helpless. It's Mascot's mission to help the helpless. Yes, if the situation were reversed, the merc would doubtless leave Mascot to be torn to shreds by a wild dog. That, however, is no excuse. What separates Mascot from the merc is that Mascot cannot turn away from someone in need . . . even if that someone is an enemy.

The dog advances on the merc, and Mascot sees the merc's fallen gun. It's just out of reach. He leaps for it, goes into a shoulder roll, and comes up holding it. It's remarkably light, not that different from the ones in his video ga—in his training room.

Mascot's sudden movement attracts the dog's notice. It turns toward him and obviously sees him as a threat. Large Lass lets out a scream as, this time, the dog bounds straight at Mascot, barking furiously, its eyes crazed. Rabies is eating its brain. The creature's obviously not long for this world; the only question is whether it's going to take Mascot with it before it goes.

Mascot never flinches. His mind flashes away from the forest, and he's back in front of his TV screen, effortlessly picking off the electronic monsters.

He levels the gun with his right hand, grips his right wrist firmly with his left hand, and fires. The *noise from the gun is far softer than he would have imagined.*

The first shot misses. The second doesn't. It strikes the charging dog squarely in its open mouth. The dog gurgles in alarm, and blood is spilling out of its maw. Mascot fires a third time, striking the dog squarely in the head. It literally flips backward through the air, blood tattooing the right half of its skull. Mascot shoots a fourth time, this time hitting the animal in the side of its body. Blood explodes from its side. The dog is covered in red. It is yelping, gasping piteously; and for half a heartbeat Mascot actually feels sorry for the thing. But that's not going to stop him from defending his friends.

He's ready to shoot again, but the dog has had enough. It turns tail and runs off into the woods, disappearing from view seconds later.

Mascot turns to the fallen merc and aims the gun at him. The merc's eyes widen.

"You go back and you tell your friends," Mascot says to him, "that I could have killed you just now. Heck, I could have let the dog kill you. But I didn't . . . because guys like Captain Major and me are better than you." Then he shoves the gun into

*his belt, adjusts his jacket to cover it, and says
briskly to Large Lass and Waistline, "Come on.
Let's go."*

*There is no subsequent feeling of terror, of near
loss, as there was when the oncoming train threatened
Large Lass. In this case Mascot was the one who
was in direct danger, and he knows that he is—for
the time being—safe. He needn't worry unless, and
until, he finds himself perched on a bridge. Until
then he knows he's going to be fine.*

*They head off in a random direction. All Mascot
wants to do at this point is get as far from the merc
as possible.*

"Josh, you . . . you were amazing back there," said
Kelsey. "I just . . . I . . . that . . . that was . . ."

"That was like watching Mascot in action," Paul said in
wonder.

Josh kept his cool, not wanting it to seem like it was any
big deal. "Just did what I had to," he said dismissively as if
it were the most routine thing in the world. "Although," he
added for Kelsey's benefit, "Mascot does stuff like that all
the time."

"I'm sure he does," Kelsey said. "So that's why, when

Josh Miller does something like that, it's a really big deal. One of the reasons he's so much easier to like than Mascot."

Josh didn't know how to respond to that, and he was relieved when Paul shouted "Look!" and pointed, thus breaking the moment. Josh and Kelsey looked in the direction that Paul was indicating.

It was the edge of the woods. There was a sidewalk visible and a row of houses across the street.

"Outstanding," said Josh.

"Yeah," Paul agreed. "It should be easy from here on in."

CHAPTER 11

THE LONG ARM
OF THE LAW

Sheriff Tom Harrelson strode into the interrogation room, where one of his deputies was seated with a shaken-looking young man dressed in what appeared to be camouflage clothes. The young man had dirty red hair that hung down around his ears, and deep-sunken eyes.

Harrelson was big, barrel-chested, with a shaved head, kind blue eyes, and infinite patience. "So what's up, Andy?" he inquired of the deputy.

Andy Cox, one of the newer additions to the

Northchester police department, said, "I thought you'd want to hear this for yourself, Sheriff. You know those kids that the guy from Wonder Comics said were on their way? I think they're here."

Harrelson frowned as he pulled a chair over, turned it around, and straddled it. "You sure? I've got our boys at the train station, the bus station. No one's reported seeing 'em. And from what I hear, the big guy with them doesn't drive."

"Well, based on what this gentleman tells me . . ."

"Why not tell *me*, Mr. . . . ?"

"Friedman. Bob Friedman." His hand gestured vaguely. "I could really use a cigarette. Can I light a cigarette?"

"Sure you can. "

Friedman started to reach for a pack in his pocket.

"But since there's a sign there that says NO SMOKING"— Harrelson pointed to the red-on-white sign on the wall— "I'd have to book you for it."

Friedman's hand dropped away from his pocket and he sighed heavily. "Okay, okay, fine."

"Mr. Friedman here came running out of Tillman Woods and nearly collided with a passing police car," said Andy.

"I see." Harrelson cleared his throat. "Well, Mr. Friedman, stumbling in front of police cars, that's kind of a problem for us. But my man Andy here seems to feel you got something worthwhile to tell us. So . . . ?" he prompted.

"Yeah, well, okay . . . so here's the thing. A bunch of friends and me were out in the forest playing paintball."

"Paintball?"

"Yeah." He shifted uncomfortably in his chair, his hand still twitching, clearly craving a cigarette. "About half a dozen of us go into the woods with paint guns and do war games. The guns shoot red paint capsules. You get hit in the arm or leg, it's a wound. In the chest, it's fatal. But the whole thing's a game; it's harmless fun."

"Really." Harrelson wasn't amused. "Funny thing, Mr. Friedman: We hereabouts in the sheriff's office don't tend to consider people running around shooting each other as 'harmless' *or* 'fun.' Guess it comes from the idea that if people shoot at us, we don't just go home and have to wash it out of our clothes, get it?"

"Yeah. I guess so," said Friedman, looking down.

"So am I to understand that you encountered some youngsters in the woods?" He looked at Andy Cox. "That where we're going with this?"

"The kid jumped me."

"Jumped you?"

"Yeah. Me and two buddies were out in the woods, and then he threw a hornet's nest at me. . . ."

"You don't look stung."

"There weren't no hornets in it. Then he jumped on me and knocked me to the ground."

"You do realize the boy is twelve. You're telling me you were beaten up by a twelve-year-old?"

"He surprised me," said Friedman defensively. "And he had two people with him . . . a big guy and some chubby girl."

"You planning to press charges?"

"Charges?" Friedman looked surprised at the idea. "Heck, Sheriff, if you find the kid, I want to shake his hand. Kid saved my life."

"By knocking you down?" Harrelson was completely confused. "I'm not following. . . ."

"You know that wild dog we heard reports of wandering the woods?" asked Cox. "The rottweiler? The one that animal control hasn't been able to find?"

"Yeah."

"Well, apparently it was worse than just wild. It was rabid . . . and it attacked Mr. Friedman here."

"The thing showed up out of nowhere," Friedman said. "I was flat on my back . . . my buddies ran off, and you can bet I'll let 'em have it for that. Anyway, dog's coming right at me, and this kid, he picks up my paint gun and, cool as a cucumber, starts shooting the thing. Drove it off."

"With a *paint gun*?"

"He didn't just drive it off, Sheriff," said Cox. "I just got a call; a routine patrol found its body. He killed the thing."

"Got a shot right down its throat," Friedman told them.

"Paint in the lungs. That would do it," said the sheriff. "Kid did us a huge favor . . . the dog, too, truth to tell. May have saved the lives of future half-drunk fools who wander around in the woods looking for trouble. So tell me, Rambo . . . where'd the boy get off to? Him and his friends?"

"I don't know. They ran off. I went back to where we'd left the car and found out the other guys had driven off."

"So your good pals left you to die and a twelve-year-old kid bailed you out."

"That's . . . pretty much right."

Harrelson had been tilting forward in his chair. Now he leaned back and stroked his chin thoughtfully. "Deputy," he said distantly, "toss Mr. Friedman here in lockup."

"Hey! You can't do that!"

"Reckless endangerment? Misuse of public lands? I'm

pretty sure I can. Deputy . . ." He tilted his head toward the door on the other side of the room. Cox took Friedman firmly by the elbow and led him out.

The sheriff stayed in the interrogation room for a few minutes, thoughtful, until Deputy Andy Cox came back in. "He's tucked away, Tommy," said Cox, instantly becoming less formal once he was alone with Harrelson. "We arresting him?"

"Nah. Not worth the paperwork. Just keep him on ice until he's dried out, then kick him loose. So . . . the woods. The woods butt up against the train station. Who've we got out there?"

"Kellerman."

"Tell Kellerman that he's got to learn to keep his eyes open. They must have slipped off the train and gone around into the woods. But they're on foot."

"If they're on foot, how are we going to find them?"

"Northchester isn't that big, Andy. If we got the whole population together—had them join hands and walk across the town in one big line—we'd find them that way."

Andy looked puzzled. "That what you want me to do?"

"Noooo . . . no. Here's what you *can* do, though. Get word out to every bus driver, every cabbie. Tell them who we're looking for. If any of them spot 'em, inform this office immediately. We have a unit over at Mr. Kirby's house?"

"Yeah."

He rose from his chair and straightened his shirt. "Tell them someone is going to come and take over for them."

"Who?"

"Me."

"You, boss? How come?"

"Because"—Harrelson smiled—"any kid who faces down a vicious dog when the adults go running away is definitely worth meeting."

CHAPTER 12

ON THE ROAD AGAIN

Much of the drive up to Northchester had been made in silence. The miles flew by, Zack watching the road carefully as the convertible sped through the Bronx and up toward Northchester. Doris leaned back, enjoying the way her hair blew in the wind. "This takes me back," she finally said.

Zack glanced over at her. "Back where?"

"My ex-husband had a convertible when he was a teenager."

"You knew him when you were kids?"

"Yup. High school sweethearts. Guess we got married too young. Anyway, back then we'd go for drives and my hair would be all over the place. Drove me crazy."

"Do you need me to pull over, put the top up?"

"No, no," she assured him. "My hair's much shorter now, and besides, I'm too old to worry about such things anymore."

She was quiet for a moment and then said something so softly that Zack didn't hear her at first, thanks to the wind snatching her words away, and asked her to repeat it. "I said, how did she die? Your wife, I mean. If you don't mind my asking. If you do, and you don't want to talk about it, I totally underst—"

"Cancer."

She winced. "I'm sorry. That . . . must have been terrible for you. And for Kelsey. I mean, obviously for your wife as well, but you're the ones who had to deal with it after she passed."

"I'm not sure how well we've been dealing," he admitted. "Kelsey . . . she wasn't really all that slim before her mom passed away, but after that she ballooned. Just so sad, I guess. Eating was how she coped with it."

"And how did you cope?"

He cast a glance at her. "I got sloppy."

"Pardon?"

"In answer to your question about coping: I got sloppy." He slowed to allow some nut in a Corvette to go speeding by. "In my work, I mean. I stopped caring. Stopped being cautious. I guess . . . I mean, I know this'll sound crazy, but maybe part of me figured, you know, if I die, then at least I'm with her again."

"But you'd be leaving Kelsey behind." Her tone was faintly scolding.

"Yeah. I know. Wasn't thinking straight. I kept throwing myself into dangerous situations, and for a while I was lucky, but eventually my luck ran out. I saw a liquor store holdup going down, and instead of radioing for backup or waiting for the perp to exit the store, I went charging in like some idiot on a TV show and tried to John Wayne the whole situation. I didn't realize he had a friend backing him up, and the friend shot me. Then when I was lying there bleeding, and I couldn't move and thought that maybe I was going to die, that's the point when it really sank in that, if I was gone, who was going to watch after Kelsey? Who'd be there for her? My goofball sister off in Alaska? My parents, both in their seventies? She needed me."

"Well . . . at least you lived to realize your mistake."

"I haven't talked to anybody about this," Zack said. "You're surprisingly easy to talk to."

"I'm full of surprises."

She slumped back, her head on the seat headrest. "Look, Zack . . . I'm sorry I didn't rein in my son more. This really is all his fault. Maybe . . . maybe we really should keep the two of them apart from now on."

"Yeah, because parents trying to keep kids from seeing each other . . . that always works," he said, smiling. "Look, I may be overprotective, and jumpy, and judgmental, and kind of harsh—but I'm not stupid. We have to set guidelines, rules . . . but . . ."

"But we have to trust our kids."

"Yes. And trust that they have the good sense to know right from wrong."

"Well . . . did you ever consider that maybe you gave Kelsey such a sense of right and wrong that, when she saw Josh was in need, she felt it would be wrong not to do everything she could to help him?"

"I . . ."

He took his eyes off the road long enough to look at her as if he were seeing her for the first time. Then he quickly went back to watching the road. "Your husband left you, huh?"

"Yup."

"Man's an idiot . . . if you don't mind my saying so."

She smiled. "I don't mind at all."

CHAPTER 13

MASCOT CORNERED

Paul was sitting on a bench in a small park, staring miserably at the children in a playground nearby. Kelsey was seated next to him, patting him reassuringly on the shoulder, while Josh crouched in front of him. "It's not your fault," Josh said.

"Yes, it is." Paul groaned. "I said I'd bring you there. But we have to take the bus. I always take the bus from the train station. But we can't get to the train station now, and I don't know where else the bus is."

"It's going to be okay. We can still work this out," Josh told him. "Look . . . you know the address, right?"

"Yes, but I'm not supposed to tell anyone. . . ."

Kelsey spoke carefully. "Okay, Paul, that's true. But you are allowed to *go* there, right? Well . . . certainly if you were lost, you could tell someone the address if they were going to take you there, couldn't you?"

"I . . ." He considered that. "I guess."

"Okay, well . . . we can take a taxi there. You tell the taxi driver where you want to go, and he can take us there."

"You really think so?" His face and mood were brightening considerably. "He'll do that?"

"Sure. Let's go."

Paul's sadness vanished, and minutes later they were walking along the street, trying to find a taxi.

It took them a little while, because Northchester was not exactly New York City, and there weren't yellow cabs cruising by the dozens. Eventually, though, they spotted a white car with a checker design running along the side, and the words MAJESTIC CABS painted on it. Kelsey raised a hand and gesticulated fiercely. The cab, which had been about to pass them by, practically screeched to a halt. The three of them bounded into it, squeezing into the backseat.

A young woman was at the wheel. She had a broad face

and a gap between her front teeth. "I thought you were
going to throw your shoulder out waving like that, young
lady."

Then she looked at the three of them. Really looked.

*Mascot is instantly suspicious. There is
something in the cab driver's face that strikes him
as odd. Almost as if she has recognized them
somehow. But that should not be possible. He is in
his secret identity, not wearing his costume or mask,
and Large Lass and Waistline are similarly in civilian
disguise.*

"We need to go to . . ." Paul glanced in either direction
at Josh and Kelsey, since he was seated between them, and
then dropped his voice to a whisper and said, "Number fifteen Mills Street."

"Got it," the cab driver whispered back.

"Mills Street?" Kelsey turned to Josh. "Josh! That has to
be where he got the last name for Mascot's secret identity!
From his own street name! See? Coincidences happen!"

Josh was barely listening. Instead, as the cab pulled
away from the curb, he was paying attention to the cab
driver. It was a little hard to hear her because there was a

plastic partition, a shield, mounted between the seats, separating the backseat from the front. She picked up a microphone attached to a squawk box and said, "Dispatcher, this is cab three, en route to fifteen Mills Street."

A voice came back from the box, and it sounded startled. "You found—?"

"*En route!*" she said, so quickly that she interrupted him.

"Right. Okay. Got you, cab three."

It's a trap! How could he have been so blind! "Majestic" cabs. A woman driver. Obviously this is a front for one of Captain Major's oldest foes, Madame Majestic.

Large Lass and Waistline don't notice. But Mascot doesn't hesitate. Immediate action must be taken.

He yanks on the door release. It doesn't open. "Unlock this right now!" he demands.

"Where do you think you're going, hon?" says the cab driver, sounding like she's his best friend in the world. Ohhh, she's good. She's very good. Smooth as glass. "We're nowhere near Mills yet."

"Pull over and let us out!"

"What's wrong?" asks Large Lass, and Waistline
is starting to look concerned.

"She's in with them! She works for Madame
Majestic!"

"Hon," says the driver, "I don't know anyone
like—"

"Tell them the truth! Right now!"

"Honey, this has really got to—"

Mascot starts hammering on the partition. "Pull
over! Now! Let us out!"

"It's for your own good," she shouts back,
dropping any pretense. "And stop hitting that! It—"

"You hear that?" Mascot shouts desperately.
"She's with the bad guys!" He continues to pound
on the shield. It shudders but holds.

"There's no bad guys! Okay, look, the police put
out an all-points on you three! They told the bus
drivers, cabbies. There's probably a police car
waiting for you at the address you're going to!
So sit down and stay—"

"We've got to get out of here, right now!"
Mascot bellows.

"You got it," says Waistline. He leans forward,
cocks his fist, and drives it forward.

The shield has no chance. Waistline knocks it right out of its frame and it falls forward, crashing down on the driver.

She lets out an alarmed yell and slams the car to a halt. A screeching of brakes tells them that a car has nearly rear-ended them. It goes around them, honking, the driver shaking his fist as he passes. Meantime, Mascot leaps forward. The driver is pressed forward under the combined weight of Mascot and the shield. She grunts, trying to sit up, but she's pinned. Mascot sees the unlock button mounted on her door. He reaches out and thumbs it, and the doors unlock.

They clamber out of the car onto the sidewalk. The driver throws open her door and shouts, "All right, you little—" Then she stops, her eyes widen. "Don't shoot me!" she suddenly cries out. She leaps back into the car, and the taxi peels out so fast that the tires leave rubber marks on the asphalt.

They were left standing in downtown Northchester. There were assorted small shops, but most of them were closed because they catered to tourists, and this wasn't tourist season.

"Don't shoot me?" said Josh, bewildered. "What was she talking ab—"

"Josh!" Kelsey pointed.

Josh looked down. His Windbreaker had ridden up in the back, and the gun butt was visible.

"You've gotta be kidding!" said Kelsey in annoyance. "Why are you still carrying that around?"

Josh pulled it out from his belt. "It's perfectly safe," he said defensively.

"It is not safe! You saw what it did to that dog. It's as *not* safe as you can *get*! If nothing else, it could go off accidentally and hurt someone, especially if you hit them in the face. You should never have taken it!"

"It's not going to go off accidentally!" Josh assured her, trying to flip it into his other hand to demonstrate his command of it.

The gun went off.

Fortunately, it was pointed at the wall of a building. A red splotch appeared on it.

"Whoops," Josh said. Then he frowned. "Why is the wall bleeding?"

"It's not bleeding, doofus. It's more red paint."

"Red . . ." He stared at his "weapon." "It's a *paint gun*?"

"Of course it's a paint gun. What, you couldn't tell? It

makes a whole different noise from regular guns."

"Sure I could tell," Josh said defensively. "So . . . those guys in the forest . . ."

"What, did you think they were really mercs?" asked Kelsey. "With paint guns? They were probably guys playing war games or something."

"No way," Josh said firmly. He turned the gun over and over, studying it. "It's just that they wanted to take us alive. Maybe the paint has radioactive trace elements that would have let them track us once we were marked. . . ."

"Josh!" Kelsey stomped her foot in irritation. "Of all the—"

She took the paint gun from his grasp and chucked it into a nearby trash can.

That was when they heard the police siren nearby.

"Aw no," said Josh.

Paul was looking extremely nervous. "I'm gonna get in so much trouble. Joe's gonna be so mad at me if I get arrested. . . ."

"Maybe they're not coming for us," said Kelsey, but she wasn't convincing anybody, even herself. For a moment she considered just giving up, but she thought of how much trouble she'd get in with her father if he found out what she'd been up to.

It had all seemed like a good idea at the time, and Josh had been so scared and so desperate and he'd needed her help. She'd figured that she could pull it off without her dad being any the wiser. If he found out . . . if she wound up being arrested and they called her dad and he had to come up to Northchester to get her . . . she'd be grounded for the rest of her life.

So when Josh shouted, "This way!" rather than do the smart thing and just wait for the police car and call it a day, she ran after him. Paul didn't hesitate; he followed right behind.

They sprinted down the street, running past assorted closed stores, including the local library, which was open only until noon during the week. They got to the corner and skidded to a halt when Josh realized to his horror that he'd messed up. The echoes had fooled him: He'd thought the police car was coming from behind them, but no. It was coming toward them.

Even from this distance, he could see that it was being driven by the police officer who'd been looking for them at the train station. And he looked reeeeeaally annoyed.

The police car obviously had a loudspeaker on it, because his voice boomed over it. "Put the gun down, kid! Put it down and put your hands over your head!"

Kelsey looked to Josh, bewildered. "How . . . how did he . . . ?"

"The cab driver must have radioed it in," said Josh.

"We already threw it away," and Kelsey . . .

. . . *is obviously about to shout that to the police officer, but Mascot suddenly takes charge. "Down that way," Mascot orders. He points to his right. "Head that way and circle back around on the other side. I'll meet you there after I draw off our pursuer."*

"What are you talking about? How are you going to do that?"

"He thinks I'm armed. I'm the one he'll come after. Look, we're out of time. He can't chase both of us, and he'll think I'm the most dangerous. Go! Go!"

Large Lass hesitates only a moment, and then she and Waistline bolt down the street. Mascot turns and runs as if his life depends on it.

His legs are a blur, scissoring as fast as they can. He doesn't have to turn around to know that the police car is following him. He can hear it.

"Hold it, son!" It is the voice of the police officer, coming over the loudspeaker. He sounds

annoyed. "Stop running!"

Mascot doesn't cooperate. He keeps going. The police car is following, although it's moving slowly now since all it has to do is keep up with a kid on foot.

He skids to a halt in front of the library and turns to face the police officer. The police car slows, stops; the officer gets out. He has not pulled his own gun; it remains holstered, but his hand is hovering near it. The expression on his face makes it clear that the last thing he wants to do is draw it. "Where's the gun, son?"

Mascot points toward the garbage can. "Down there. We already tossed it, and anyway it was just a paint gun."

The cop lets out a sigh. "It _was_ the one from those idiots in the woods. Okay, _that's_ a relief. Now come on, son . . . there's plenty of people worried about you and your friends."

Mascot almost feels sorry for him. The cop cannot possibly know that he is being manipulated by forces beyond his understanding—evil supervillains who have conspired to drive a wedge between two of the foremost fighters for good and the forces of

the law. When all this is over, and Captain Major
and Mascot have triumphed—as they inevitably
will—Mascot is going to be sure to send the police
officers a nice gift. Maybe a box of cookies or
something like that.

"All right now, son," says the cop.

"Stop calling me 'son,'" Mascot says angrily.
"I'm not your son."

"Okay. Fine." He no longer has his hand near
his gun as he walks toward Mascot. "Now . . .
enough's enough. There's a lot of people worried
about you."

Oh, most certainly there are. The assembled
hordes of bad guys must be terrified that Mascot will
somehow survive their perfidi . . . their prefiedi . . .
their evil plans. They're doubtless hoping that
Mascot will now surrender. In doing so, he'll make
himself an easy target, locked in a jail cell that they
can turn into a death trap with no problem.

"Sorry," Mascot says airily. "Time for me to
book."

He spins and grabs the large metal drawer that's
built into the wall of the library behind him: the
deposit slot where people can return books when the

library is closed. Fortunately the town made it extra large so it would be easier to return oversize art books or even stacks of books. Even more fortunately, Mascot is very thin, and very bendable. He yanks it open and slides in.

The cop yells and covers the remaining distance between them in a few quick strides. Mascot's front half slides in easy enough, but before he can yank his legs through, the cop grabs his ankle. Mascot is squirming furiously, however, and he manages to kick free before the cop can get a solid hold. He slides through the slot and tumbles headfirst into a cart that's been set up to catch returned books. The cart tumbles over, spilling Mascot and several recently returned volumes to the floor.

He hears a pounding on the front glass doors. He sees the police officer standing there, thudding his fists furiously and shouting something. Mascot guesses that it's nothing flattering. The cop yanks on the doors, but they remain securely locked. He yells in frustration, but the sound is muffled. Mascot has a feeling that the Comics Code Authority wouldn't approve some of the words the police officer is shouting.

Mascot turns and dashes across the library floor. There is, just as he'd hoped, a back door. It's locked from the outside in, but nothing's preventing him from heading out. There's a large push bar across the middle, and he shoves against it without slowing down. The door springs open, and Mascot bounds into the street on the other side of the building.

He looks around frantically, trying to spot Large Lass and Waistline. There's no sign of them. For a heartbeat he panics, worried that they may be in the clutches of the forces of evil. . . .

"Josh!"

Josh didn't see where the voice was coming from at first, and then he spotted it. Directly across the street, in front of a pizza parlor, there was a small cargo van with the pizza parlor's logo on the side. Obviously it was a delivery van. The back doors were open. He couldn't see Kelsey, but her hand was sticking out, waving frantically.

Josh glanced right and left and then dashed across the street. He clambered into the back of the van and swung the doors shut behind them.

Paul and Kelsey were crouched inside. They were a

tight fit, but it was manageable. They stayed where they were, not moving, hardly daring to breathe. They heard the police siren coming around the corner. Kelsey and Paul both looked frightened, and it was everything Josh could do to maintain what he hoped was a look of focused, steely resolve. The police siren approached and came right near them . . . and then kept going. It sailed on down the street and soon was receding into the distance.

They let out a collective sigh.

"Okay, so now what?" asked Kelsey.

"We get out and get to Stan Kirby."

"How?" Paul said.

Josh tried to come up with something, but his mind was blank. Buses, cabs, every regular method of transport was closed to them. They could walk, but Paul didn't seem to have a clear idea of how to get there on foot, and the chances of the police spotting them were huge.

Paul sighed and leaned back against the inside of the truck. "Too bad we're not pizzas. We could just get ourselves delivered there."

"Yeah," said Kelsey, "we'd just call in and get brought . . . there. . . ."

Her voice trailed off as Josh's eyes widened. So did Kelsey's.

"That's brilliant," said Josh. "That's . . . that's brilliant."

"There's a pay phone just down the corner," said Kelsey, grabbing at her pockets. "I've got change. The phone number is on the front of the building."

"I don't understand," Paul said, looking confused. "What are we doing? What's going on?"

"You just came up with a brilliant plan to get us to Stan Kirby," Josh said cheerfully as Kelsey handed him a fistful of quarters. "We should be there in thirty minutes or less. And hey . . . if we're not, we're free."

Paul blinked, trying to take in what Josh had just told him. He had come up with a plan. And the plan he had come up with was brilliant. Josh had said it three times: Brilliant.

His confusion melted away like morning frost in the hot sun. He squared his shoulders and grinned, ready for whatever came next.

CHAPTER 14

SPECIAL DELIVERY

Sheriff Tom Harrelson pulled up at curbside next to Stan Kirby's house in an unmarked car. He killed the engine and slumped down so as to attract minimal attention. He had a clear view of the street in front of him and, using his rearview mirror, could keep tabs on everything behind him.

His officers had been keeping him apprised of everything that was going on via radio, and he was having trouble believing what he was hearing. Bad enough that these kids had given them the slip at the train station. Then they'd taken care of dispatching a vicious dog that the police had not been able to track down. Now this Josh kid had yet again managed to outthink one of his men by escaping through a closed library. This after being caught briefly by a cab driver from whom they'd gotten away, and who'd panicked at the sight of a supposed weapon: a paint gun the kid had obviously secured from those idiots sprinting around in the woods. By the time the police officer had gotten back to his squad car and driven around the block, the kid and his pals had vanished once more.

This was beyond ridiculous. This was getting embarrassing.

At the same time, Harrelson had to feel a degree of grudging admiration for the kid. The boy seemed to have an endless supply of guts and ingenuity. When Josh was old enough, Harrelson was thinking, he'd try to recruit him for the sheriff's office. Heck, maybe he should just sign him up now. Better to be with the kid than against him.

And now the sheriff had just been informed that the two youngsters' parents had come to town. They had shown up at the sheriff's office, apparently hoping to discover that the kids had been rounded up, and were none too pleased to discover that they were still running loose. The sheriff couldn't blame them. They'd departed the sheriff's office, clearly annoyed. The deputy had tried to make them stay put, but they hadn't done anything wrong; he couldn't exactly arrest them simply for being concerned parents. Harrelson had every reason to suppose that they had Kirby's address in hand and were on their way over. The one saving grace in all this was that the girl's dad was apparently a police officer, so at least Harrelson would be dealing with one experienced hand instead of two panicky parents.

The one person who hadn't been brought up to speed on this whole thing was Stan Kirby himself. Harrelson was hoping to have the entire matter resolved without disturbing him. Kirby was an unpredictable cuss. Even after all these years, Harrelson was still a bit intimidated by him. This man had been single-handedly responsible for some of the fondest memories that Harrelson had of his childhood. That kind of respect, even awe, tended to stay with you no matter how old you got.

Harrelson heard the sound of a car approaching from behind and glanced in his rearview. It was a pizza delivery van. Apparently Kirby was ordering in.

He watched as the pizza van made a right turn and

pulled into Stan Kirby's driveway. It glided right up to the garage and then stopped. The pizza kid stepped out of the driver's side, walked around to the passenger side, and pulled out a pizza wrapped in a large insulated bag.

Giving the routine pizza delivery no more thought, Harrelson went back to watching the street. These kids were smart and might take advantage of Harrelson being distracted by a delivery to try to sneak past him. Well, that just wasn't going to happen, no sir. Not on Harrelson's watch.

The pizza delivery guy was named Dennis. At that moment Dennis was completely bewildered as an annoyed voice from the other side of the door said, "What pizza? I didn't order a pizza!"

Dennis checked the order slip that was dangling from the box. The address was right. "You Mr. Kirby?" he called.

"What's it to you?"

"That's the name on the order, and this is the right address."

"Look, kiddo, whatever you're selling, I'm not buying. And if you think I'm opening this door so you can stick your foot in and stop me from closing it until I pay you for a pizza I never ordered, or listen to you telling me about whoever your personal God is or whatever your angle is, you can just forget it! You hear me?"

Dennis knew when it was time to give up. "Fine, mister. Fine. Whatever. I'm leaving, okay?"

"Good!"

Shaking his head and not wanting to think what the boss at the pizza parlor was going to say, Dennis stalked back to his van, the pizza box slung under his arm. He tossed it carelessly onto the passenger seat and then noticed something unusual: The back doors of the van were hanging open. He went around back and looked in. There was nothing inside. No reason that there should have been: Dennis used the back section of the van only when he was transporting a large number of pizzas for a big party or catering job, something like that.

"Weird," he muttered. He grabbed the doors and slammed them shut. He checked to make sure they were secure and then climbed into the driver's side. Dennis stared at the pizza, grunted in annoyance, flipped open the lid, took out a slice, and ate it. If he was going to be yelled at—which he probably was, even though it wasn't remotely his fault—he might as well have a full stomach.

Stan Kirby watched through the peephole in his front door, making sure that the guy from the pizza place was going back to his van and driving off.

"Probably some kind of prank," he muttered. Certainly that had to be it. Some idiot kid had thought it would be funny to fake order a pizza and have it delivered. Well, he didn't have time to give it any thought. He had a deadline to meet.

He turned and stopped dead in his tracks.

There were three people standing in the hallway behind him. One of them he recognized immediately: It was that guy from the office. Pat? Paul? Something like that. Harmless enough, although Kirby couldn't say he was ecstatic that the guy was sneaking in through the back door. But there were two kids with him, a boy and a girl. The girl was looking at him with open curiosity, and the boy . . . well, he looked stunned, as if someone had just hit him across the face with a two-by-four.

"What are you doing here? What do you want?" demanded Kirby.

"Mr. Kirby," said the office guy, gesturing toward the boy, "this young man needs to talk to you."

The boy took a step forward even though his legs were wobbling. Then his eyes rolled up into the top of his head and he fainted dead away.

CHAPTER 15

MASCOT MEETS HIS MAKER

When Josh and the others had clambered out of the back of the van as quietly as they could, Josh had found himself almost paralyzed with alarm. He spotted the car seated at curbside and the man in the passenger seat, and although the car had no markings on it and he couldn't see the man clearly, he had been certain it was the police on stakeout. Fortunately the guy was looking away from them. Josh's brain sent desperate signals to his feet. The notion of getting so close to his goal and then being stopped short of it nearly overwhelmed him. Then Kelsey helped out by giving him a good hard shove. It made him stumble slightly but he recovered fast. Paul was already moving quickly, waving for them to follow. Since Paul had been there any number of times, he was the best one to show them how to get into the house.

Arriving at the back door, Paul tentatively turned the doorknob. The door was unlocked.

They entered the kitchen. The top edges of the sink were stained, and there were dishes piled up. A slow, steady drip was coming from the faucet. The cabinets desperately needed a coat of paint. The oven in the corner looked positively ancient, and the linoleum was yellowing.

Josh was confused. He had been expecting something way more high-tech, similar to what Captain Major had in the Secret Sanctum. This was more run-down than his kitchen back home.

Kelsey was wrinkling her nose. Josh couldn't blame her.

Paul gestured for them to follow. They moved through the kitchen into a hallway. Josh glanced off to his left and suddenly stopped.

There was a room with the door open.

It was an art studio.

There was a drawing board, the surface of which was

covered with black stains. Pages of artwork, ten-by-fifteen bristol board, were piled all over the place.

This was where the magic happened. This was where Captain Major came to life.

Josh forgot to breathe, he was so stunned at what he was seeing.

"What are you doing here? What do you want?" came an angry voice. Josh's head whipped around.

Stan Kirby wasn't remotely like what he had imagined. He had figured Stan Kirby would be six feet tall, square jawed, with a head of thick blond hair and keen, glittering eyes that took in everything around him. He would speak with a deep, booming voice that quaked like thunder. He would look like a superhero.

Instead Stan Kirby was an old man.

He was maybe a head taller than Josh himself. And he was stooped, like someone who had been hunched over a drawing board his entire life. His hair was a buzz cut, black on the sides but gray on top. He was peering over a pair of thick glasses and was wearing faded blue jeans and a red-and-black plaid shirt. His Adam's apple bobbed visibly in his throat.

This couldn't be Stan Kirby.

"Mr. Kirby," said Paul, destroying that sole remaining

hope, "this young man needs to talk to you."

Josh tried to become Mascot. He tried to send his mind to that place where Mascot's inner narrative kicked in. He could be quicker, smarter, better than anyone, and he could come up with some sort of scenario that would explain this . . . this crushing disappointment.

But Mascot wouldn't come to him.

Trapped in the real world, he was overcome with exhaustion and his brain shut down. Everything went black. He was vaguely aware that something hard had hit him, and then he realized it was the floor, and that was the last thing he remembered.

They think they have Mascot trapped . . .
helpless. But they are wrong, so very wrong.
Mascot struggles mightily as they try to shove
the truth serum down his throat.

Josh spit out the water and almost choked as he did so. "Whoa, whoa!" came Stan Kirby's voice, and the world began to refocus itself.

He realized he was lying on a couch in Kirby's living room. The couch was kind of beat-up, and there was mustiness in the air. Stan Kirby was crouched next to him, with Paul and Kelsey standing nearby, looking concerned.

Kirby remained gruff, but he no longer seemed hostile. "Gave us a little bit of a scare there, sport," he said. "Here. Try to keep this down."

Josh sat up and, taking the glass, drank the water. It was cold going down his throat, and tasted slightly rusty.

"Sorry," he managed to say.

"So," said Kirby, standing. "From what Paul tells me, you've had quite an adventure getting up here . . . all because you think . . . what? That you're going to die when Mascot dies?"

"Yes! Yes, exactly. I need you not to do it."

Kirby snorted and adjusted his glasses. "You got some imagination, sport. You ought to be writing comic books."

"I have. I do. I write them. I draw them. Do you . . ." He hesitated. Despite the fact that Kirby was not remotely what he had expected, nevertheless this man was still a god in the world of comics. "Do you have any advice?"

"Yeah. Stop. Before it's too late."

Josh gaped at him. He was speechless. Kelsey stepped in. "Why would you tell him to do that? I mean, it's what you do, and you're great at it. . . ."

"*Great?*" Kirby guffawed at that. "You think what I do is great? Great, kid, is what hangs in the Louvre or the

Museum of Modern Art. Great is material that speaks to you from the very bottom of your soul. What I do? It's junk. Commercial, disposable garbage aimed at . . . well, at kids like you."

Josh was shaking his head, feeling stunned. "That's . . . that's not true."

"Yeah, it is, kid." Kirby actually sounded regretful for a moment. "Look, you want me to blow sunshine up your skirt?"

"I'm not wearing a skirt. . . ."

"You want me to tell you what you want to hear? I can't do that. I'm too old, I'm too tired, and I got no reason to pretend that what I do means anything. I mean . . . I don't get you," and he sat on the couch a few feet away from Josh. "When I was your age, I had so many things I wanted to do in my life. So many dreams. I dreamed about my art hanging in great museums. I dreamed about doing stuff that mattered. I never dreamed of . . . of this comic book tripe. Where are your dreams that matter?"

"You gave me the *only* dreams that matter."

"Aw, geez," moaned Kirby, slumping back and covering his face with his hands. "Who *says* stuff like that?"

"People who read your comics, I guess," Paul suggested.

Josh was reeling, looking as if someone had repeatedly punched him in the face. Kelsey said, "Mr. Kirby, with all due respect, I don't think even you believe all the things you're saying. Josh says you've been doing comics for years and years and years. I just don't think that someone could put that much of his life into creating something that he can't stand."

Kirby was silent for a long moment, and it seemed that something in his face softened. "Look . . . I admit it was . . . well, kind of fun, at first. Harmless entertainment. But as time went on . . ." He shook his head.

"As time went on, what?" prodded Kelsey.

"The comics changed. The audience changed. It wasn't innocent, wide-eyed kids who just loved the heroes being heroic. Kids were off playing video games or hanging out on the internet or whatnot, and the books were aimed at cynical grown-ups. Grown-ups who wanted to see grown-up ideas in stories that should have remained just kid stuff. You know when it really hit home for me? I was in one of those comic book shops. I was driving by and I figured, what the heck, and I stopped and went in. The guy behind the counter didn't recognize me, which was fine. And a father wandered in with his kid, who couldn't have been more than seven or eight. He asked what comic would be appropriate for his son. You know what? The guy behind the counter didn't have any. Everything was filled with blood and violence. There's no place for my kind of comic books anymore."

"But that's not true," Josh protested. "I love your comics! I love Mascot! How can you be killing him?"

"That's the point, sport. I'm not killing him. The readers are. That shows just how far downhill it's all gone. They can't stand the thought of something pure and innocent and heroic; they need to tear it down. Now, I'm willing to believe that maybe you're the exception. But there's just not enough of you around. In fact, you may be the only one. And fess up: Would you be as worried about Mascot dying if you didn't believe that what happens to him will also happen to you? Look, sport, the fact of the matter is, sales on *Captain Major* have been tanking for years." Kirby stood up and paced the living room. "He's too 'old school.' Mike Galton, he told me to do something to spice up sales, so I came up with Mascot. Kid sidekicks always used to work. Not anymore. Now people hate them. Kid readers used to identify with them; now it's all grown-up readers, who talk about how stupid it is that an adult would endanger a child by dragging him into dangerous situations. So with sales still dropping, Mike came up with the idea of having a contest to decide whether Mascot lives or dies. I okayed it because by that point, frankly, I didn't care anymore. I feel like I got nothing more to offer."

Mascot almost wants to break down and cry.

After a long and agonizing search, here is Captain Major himself. But everything that he's gone through, the fact that the people have turned against him . . . it has brought him lower than Mascot has ever seen him.

"You're wrong," Mascot tells him.

The Captain just shakes his head wearily. "I wish I were."

"I know you are. There are still people out there who believe in you. I know, because I'm one of them. What would this world be like if we didn't have heroes to try to imitate? In fact . . . you know what? That's what makes people heroes. Heroes aren't the ones who keep fighting when everyone is telling them they should. Heroes are the ones who keep fighting even when everyone is telling them they shouldn't. The things you say and do and stand for . . . they mean a lot to a lot of people and to a lot of kids like me."

"There aren't a lot of kids like you," says Captain Major. *"Believe me, sport, I wish there were."*

"How will there ever be if you abandon us? The only way things can change is if guys like you and guys like me change them."

"You talk a good game, sport. But in the end, sometimes you just have to know when to quit."

"I know when to quit. It's when I'm dead," Mascot says defiantly. *"And not one minute before. You taught me that. You and all the adventures that I've had, thanks to you."*

Stan Kirby gave Josh a sidelong glance and then said to Kelsey, "Okay, is he . . . doing the thing you said where he's pretending to be Mascot now, or is this really him talking?"

Kelsey shrugged. "Hard for me to know sometimes."

"Look, sport,"—and Kirby patted him on the shoulder—"you've been good for some laughs, I'll give you that. But what's done is done. Which reminds me." He kept talking before Josh could jump in with another speech. "You. Paul. You going back to the office?"

"Yessir."

"Then you can save me a trip to the shipping place. I got the whole issue done. Can you take it back for me?

We're running late enough as it is."

"Sure, Mr. Kirby."

Josh slumped on the couch like a stringless marionette while Kirby went into the studio to get the pages. Kelsey reached over and put her hand atop Josh's. It felt cold to her. "You did your best," she whispered.

"Doing your best doesn't mean anything unless it's good enough," he replied. He sounded as if his voice was coming from the other side of a canyon.

Kirby emerged from the studio with a portfolio. He paused in front of the coffee table and then said to Josh, not ungently, "Do you want to see it?"

"I thought it was done," Kelsey said. "There were preview pages up on the internet."

"They only had a few pages of the book at the office, and it's all early draft stuff anyway. They sent it back; wanted me to do some more work on them. Make it . . ." He hesitated, as if afraid to upset Josh, and then shrugged. "Make it more graphic."

"Graphic?" Josh echoed.

"Gorier," said Kelsey. "He means gorier. Right?"

"Like I said, welcome to the modern age of comic books. Here."

He set the large portfolio down in front of Josh,

opened the black case so that the first page of the stack was visible, and gestured toward it. "There. Go ahead. Look through it if you want."

At first Josh didn't even want to touch it, but then his curiosity got the better of him. Slowly, deliberately, he read each art board and then moved it aside and started on the next one.

"See, sport?" said Kirby. "You may think that there's some sort of . . . magical connection between you and Mascot. But that's all it is, right there. Pencil and ink on bristol board. And I did it all myself, without a Magic 8-Ball or a fortune-teller. There is such a thing as coincidence, you know."

Josh continued to say nothing. Finally he got to the part that showed Mascot plummeting to his death from the bridge. Kelsey waited for him to react, to flinch, maybe even puke. He didn't do anything. It was like someone had flipped a light switch in his head and his personality had gone dark.

And then he said something very, very softly. "I thought," Josh said, speaking with effort, "that maybe it would turn out that Captain Major was Mascot's father. I wanted to believe that."

"Why?" asked Kirby, puzzled.

"Because . . ." He restacked the pages carefully and zippered up the portfolio. "I guess because . . . because I figured that Mascot's life was so much like my own, and if Captain Major was Mascot's father, then maybe my own dad . . ." Tears started to roll down his face, and he wiped them away with his sleeve. "Maybe my own dad wasn't just some rotten creep who ditched Mom and me, but maybe instead he was some big hero who was out doing amazing things. And maybe he might come back for me someday and train me to be just like him instead of . . . instead of what I am."

There were a lot of things that Stan Kirby could have said at that moment that might have made Josh feel better. But Stan Kirby was a lonely man who long ago had been hurt by someone he loved and had never really gotten over it. Which is why all he could think of to say to Josh was "Grow up, sport."

There was a knock at the door. "Wait here," said Kirby. "If it's another pizza, I'm gonna make the delivery kid wear it."

Sheriff Tom Harrelson stood before Stan Kirby's front door with his thumbs hitched into his belt. Zack Markus and Doris Miller were standing on either side of him.

"I'm doing this against my better judgment," Harrelson warned them. "I was hoping not to get Mr. Kirby worked up over this."

"He's producing a comic book that got my son so upset, he ran away from home," Doris Miller said. "I think Mr. Kirby is entitled to get just as worked up as any of us."

"Yeah?" came from the other side of the door.

"Mr. Kirby, it's Sheriff Harrelson. Mind if I come in? We have a bit of a situation."

"Yeah? I bet I know what it is."

The door swung open and Stan Kirby squinted in the late-afternoon sunlight. He glanced right and left and said, "Lemme guess: You're their parents."

Doris looked at the sheriff. "I thought you said he didn't know."

"They're in here."

"*In there?*" Harrelson couldn't believe it. "How in the world did they do that?"

"I dunno. I looked up and there they were."

"Well, they've been giving my entire department fits. May we come in?"

Kirby stepped aside and gestured for them to enter.

"*Dad?*"

It was Kelsey's voice, and Zack almost sagged in relief

the moment he heard it. It was coming from just ahead, in the living room, and sure enough, there was Kelsey, and there was the tall kid who had helped them. Kelsey looked astounded and afraid, and the tall kid just looked uncertain, and . . .

"Where's the boy?" Harrelson said, his gaze darting around the room.

"He's right over—" Kelsey started to reply, and she turned and pointed behind her.

There was no sign of Josh. There was, however, the banging of the back door, as if someone had just darted through it.

"Aw, crap," said Kirby.

"*You let him get away?!*" Doris cried out.

"I didn't *let* him do anything, lady!" Kirby snapped back. "He just—"

"Oh my gosh," said Kelsey, and she was looking at the empty coffee table. "The next issue of Captain Major. It's gone. Josh took the pages."

CHAPTER 16

THE LAST STAND

He has them. Mascot has the plans: the supersecret plans that will prove beyond a doubt that Captain Major has been framed. The plans that further describe the enemy's endgame, designed to result in the final, ultimate, for-all-time death of Captain Major and his faithful sidekick, Mascot.

Incredible that they were sitting there, right under Captain Major's nose. Only one explanation for *it: The Captain has himself been brainwashed by the enemy. Mascot is the only person thinking clearly in the whole town. It's up to him to do what must be done . . . as soon as he can figure out what that might be.*

Fortunate for him that his trusty Mascotcycle is nearby. It's waiting there, gleaming and ready for him. He leaps astride it, guns it, and tears away from the scene.

"Daaaaaaad!" cried Bobby Flannagan, who lived two doors down from Stan Kirby. He ran into the den, gesturing wildly, causing his father to knock over a house of cards he'd been meticulously stacking.

"What is it?" demanded his father, picking up the cards.

"Some kid just ran up outa nowhere and stole my bike right outa the backyard!"

The cards forgotten, his father ran to the front door and threw it open just in time to see some kid hurtle away down the driveway on his son's bike. "Get back here, you little thief!" he shouted. "*Helllp! Police!*"

There was the howl of a siren. A second later a blue sedan with a flashing police light sitting atop it roared in pursuit of the cyclist.

"Wow. That was fast," muttered Bobby's dad.

Stan Kirby and Paul were in the backseat of the sheriff's car, while Doris and Zack were in Zack's car with Kelsey. Tom Harrelson, having placed a siren atop the car, was barking alerts into his radio, letting every unit in the area know that he was in pursuit of the runaway kid who had been raising so much havoc in their town.

Josh didn't give them a backward glance. He had the portfolio case slung over his back and was pedaling as fast as he could go. He whipped around a corner. There were teenagers in the street playing stickball. They saw him coming and stepped aside, and as they did so, Josh yelled, *"The cops are chasing me and I didn't do anything wrong!"*

Seconds later, when the pursuing car zipped around the corner, the kids were standing right there, knocking the ball around. They looked up blandly as if they were unaware that a police car was coming and did nothing to get out of the way.

"Oh, for crying out loud!" shouted Harrelson. He turned hard to the right, and the car veered away from the kids and went up on the curb. The right wheels rode up for

a moment and then thudded down as he went past the teens, who were obviously snickering. Zack Markus's car followed right behind him.

Harrelson knew who every one of those kids' parents were and made a mental note to have a talk with them.

Mascot hurtles into the business district. There's more traffic. He has to be careful. This is getting tight.

There's an intersection just up ahead. The light is red for him. Two large trucks, one transporting beer, the other soda, are entering the intersection from either direction.

The wail of the police siren behind him causes the two trucks to come to a halt, which causes the traffic behind them to come to a halt, too.

There is a gap about a foot wide between the two facing trucks.

Mascot never slows. He hears a distant, alarmed shriek that remarkably rises above the siren—a woman's—and then he darts right between the two metal behemoths. He is through to the other side and is still moving, even as the police car slows to a halt. "Move the trucks!" a voice, obviously his pursuer's, shouts over a built-in loudspeaker. "Back them up, move them forward, whatever, but get out of the way!"

Mascot isn't waiting around.

He's barreling down the street, putting more distance between himself and the cop car with every passing second . . .

. . . and suddenly another one zips out of a side street, right in his path.

Mascot angles around it quickly, almost too quickly. His bike skids. He nearly tumbles off, his foot actually touching the ground, and then he rights himself and keeps going. The police car is after him.

At the last second, Mascot sees an alley between two buildings off to his right. He hangs a sharp turn that again almost causes him to be thrown from his cycle, but he catches his balance and shoots down the alley. It's too narrow for the cop car.

He practically leaps out onto the street—and for crying out loud, there's the first car that was pursuing him. How did it get here so fast? They must be coordinating their attack. Perhaps Misstermind is controlling them using her telepathy.

He angles hard to the left and keeps pedaling. He has never moved this quickly in his life. The car is closing in. The sound of the sirens is deafening.

He sees a barbershop with the door sitting wide open. Quickly Mascot heads toward it, hurtling right into the barbershop. The barber is cutting someone's hair, and he lets out a startled yell. Mascot maneuvers through the barbershop and out the back door. It opens onto a small, narrow alley. He hears the howling of the siren in the distance, but that doesn't slow him. He speeds down the alley, and it opens out onto a back street.

And _another_ police car seems to materialize out of nowhere.

It's coming from behind him, moving fast, and Mascot's legs are a blur, he's pedaling so fast.

Now there's a string of cars pursuing him, and he's starting to get tired. His breath is flagging in his chest, and sweat is dripping from his forehead into his eyes, blurring his vision.

He hears the sound of traffic, lots of it. It's coming from just down the street. Maybe, if there's a traffic tie-up, he can quickly weave his way between the standing vehicles and lose the pursuers that way.

He cuts hard to the right, heading in the direction

of the noise. He's rewarded with the sounds of screeching tires behind him as the cars in pursuit try to course correct. It takes them a moment for them to do so, and that's all the time he needs to put some more distance between himself and them.

The road ahead has narrowed to two lanes. He skids to a halt.

Dead ahead of him: A bridge. More specifically, a traffic overpass, built to provide access over the multilane Hutchinson River Parkway. Six busy lanes of traffic are speeding past in either direction far below. The parkway itself is accessible if one is willing to slide down the steep grass-covered embankment that leads to it . . . but who in his right mind would want to?

Mascot's blood freezes, but only for a moment. Then he guns the cycle forward. This is his way out. He speeds toward the overpass as fast as he can go. There is a narrow sidewalk on either side of the overpass for pedestrians, but at the moment there are no cars coming in the opposite direction. So he stays in the street, practically flying.

The way in front of him is clear. There is an intersection on the other side of the bridge. If he can get to that, he can—

A police car, lights flashing, whips around the corner from the intersection ahead of him. It roars forward, and then the cop driving it cuts the steering wheel hard. The back end of the cop car fishtails, and the car skids to a halt lengthwise across the bridge, blocking any possible exit.

Mascot jams on the handbrakes, stopping so hard that he almost causes the back wheel to flip over. He looks right, left, desperately trying to see a means of going forward. There's nothing. He jumps the cycle in a 180-degree turn, ready to head back the way he came.

Too late. Cop cars there as well.

He's trapped.

On the bridge.

Destiny is calling him, but he swears he will not go down without a fight.

Stan Kirby let out a low whistle of amazement when he saw where Josh had wound up making his last stand. "Holy cow," he muttered, peering through the front windshield of the sheriff's car. "I'm starting to wonder if maybe the kid's onto something."

Sheriff Tom Harrelson wasn't listening. Instead he was clambering out of the car, and he was hauling an electronic megaphone out from under the front seat. Paul got out of the backseat and then turned to help Kirby out.

Behind them Zack's car rolled to a halt as well. Doris Miller climbed right out of the convertible, which still had its top down, and she was screaming Josh's name. She looked frantic, out of her mind with worry.

"Everybody stay back!" shouted Sheriff Harrelson. "*Everybody!*"

Josh was standing in the middle of the bridge. He had unslung the portfolio from his back, and he was unzipping it. Despite the dire straits of the situation, he didn't appear the least bit fazed by any of it. Of everybody there, he was the calmest, which was pretty impressive considering—as far as Josh was concerned—he was fighting for his life.

All the various police officers and deputies did as they were told. Harrelson brought his megaphone up and called, "Josh! Josh Miller! This is Sheriff Harrelson."

"Hey, Sheriff," Josh called back. He sounded calm. On the other hand, Harrelson was accustomed to gauging someone's true state of mind from his eyes. Even from this distance he could see Josh's eyes, darting around frantically. That spoke far more loudly to the sheriff than Josh's voice. It told him that the boy was on the edge of panicking.

"Josh, how about you come over here and we can talk all this out. Your mother's pretty worried about you."

"I'm sorry about that. I'm sorry you're worried, Ma," he called so that his voice carried to her. "But I'm worried about me, too! I'm worried that if this comic gets published—"

"I know, Josh!" Doris called back to him. "You think you're going to die, too! But you won't, honey! I swear!"

"I sure won't!" Josh replied. *"Stay where you are!"* He shouted that when he saw the sheriff and his mother starting to approach. And he ran to the edge of the bridge, leaning against the handrail. His mother cried out in fear but she stopped moving, as did the sheriff. Holding the sides of the portfolio tightly, he held it out over the Hutchinson River Parkway. "If anybody comes any closer, the comic book gets it!"

The sheriff lowered his megaphone and considered the situation. "Okay . . . as far as threats go, that's a new one. At least he's not threatening to jump."

"Of *course* he's not threatening to jump!" Stan Kirby said in irritation, losing patience with Harrelson. "The whole point is that he feels like he's fighting for his life.

Why would someone throw himself off a bridge if he'd just gone to all this trouble to keep living?" Without waiting for Harrelson to frame a reply, Kirby stuck out his hand and said, "Give me that thing."

Harrelson hesitated but then handed Kirby the megaphone. Kirby brought it up to his mouth and pressed the talk button. "What're you planning on doing there, sport?" he asked.

"I'm sorry, Mr. Kirby," Josh said. He kept the portfolio dangling, partly unzipped, over the bridge. "I have to do this. . . ."

These plans for detonating every nuclear missile in America's arsenal cannot be allowed to fall into the wrong hands. . . .

"No, sport, you really don't."

"If this comic book gets printed, I'm done!" Josh told him with conviction. "And if you come toward me, then I . . . I swear I'll dump it! I swear. . . ."

If the villains get their hands on the formula in these documents, they'll unleash a virus that will annihilate every superhero in the world. . . .

"Well, sport," Kirby said slowly, "I don't think you really want to do that."

"Of course I do! You think I went through all this, came this far . . ."

> It has to be done and done now, because if the villains get their hands on this vital information, it will give them all the back-door codes to every business computer in the world and they can bring the entire financial market crashing to . . .

"I think," Kirby told him, "that if what you were planning to do was destroy the art . . . then you would have done it. There's no reason for you to try to keep us away from you by *threatening* to trash the artwork. Not if you really want to trash it. We're too far away from you: You could just dump it all down below and let cars run over it and destroy it all, and your job is done, right? Except . . . here's the thing . . . you *don't* really want to do that. Because coming up here and trying to get me to change my mind, well, that's one thing. But stealing another man's property, destroying it . . . that's something else again. That's not what heroes do, is it, Josh?" He paused and then said, "Is it . . . Mascot?"

Josh hesitated. "I . . ."

"You know the answer," Kirby said gently. "You know that's what the bad guys do. Don't you get it? If you act like one of the bad guys, then no one can tell you apart *from* the bad guys."

Mascot knows he must . . .
Mascot decides to . . . to . . .
Mascot . . .

"Heroes," Kirby said patiently, "put ideals above everything. They risk everything *for* ideals. You say you believe in heroism. You say you love comics. Well, you know what, Mascot? *Saying* stuff is all well and good, but the measure of a hero is what he *does*. And what you're doing, here, now . . . it's not heroic. It's just not. And all these people standing here"—he gestured toward the policemen and the spectators who seemed to have sprung up from everywhere—"you tell them you're Mascot, and they're not gonna believe you. They're just going to think you're some kid with a way overactive imagination. But me . . . you tell me you're Mascot, and I'm willing to keep an open mind. You gotta prove it to me, though . . . and doing what you're doing, well . . . if you want to prove to me you're anything but a hero, then you just go right ahead and dump the pages. Go ahead. Let's see how much of a hero you really are."

He lowered the megaphone, folded his arms across his chest, and waited. He realized that Josh's mother was standing on one side of him and Kelsey's father on the other.

"Nice speech," commented Doris Miller. "You should be a writer."

"That's what a lot of people say," said Kirby.

Josh stood there for what seemed years with, literally, his life in his hands.

It would have been so easy, so darned easy, to send the pages crashing down to the parkway. If he did that, then Mascot would be saved. He would be saved.

What should I do?

He waited for Mascot's internal narrative voice to reply, to give him guidance. Nothing came.

Surrounded by people, he was alone.

For the second time that day . . . and maybe forever . . . Mascot had deserted him.

Perhaps that was because, if he continued on this course . . . if he destroyed the artwork, destroyed that which Kirby had put so much time and effort into . . . then he didn't really deserve to be Mascot in the first place.

He was still holding the portfolio over the edge. He could see the pages within through the open section.

He let out a long, heavy sigh.

"Okay," he called. "Fine."

He started to haul the portfolio back to his side of the railing.

That was when the truck came barreling down the parkway.

Despite what the comic book pages showing Mascot's death had depicted, Josh knew that trucks weren't allowed on parkways. They're too tall, and not all the overpasses are built high enough to let them past. He once heard about some trucker getting his rig stuck under an overpass.

That wasn't happening with this truck, though. It was big—a moving truck—but it wasn't so big that it couldn't get under the overpass that he was standing on. At least, Josh didn't think so. But the nearer it got, the less sure Josh was.

It was going to be real, real close.

And the truck was moving real, real fast.

Just as Josh was starting to pull the portfolio out of harm's way, the truck barreled right under the overpass. The first thing that happened was that a massive gust of wind was generated by the truck's approach, and the second thing was that the top of the trailer ripped up the underside of the overpass. The noise was so loud, so earsplitting, that Josh was startled. The violent shaking of the overpass from the impact threw Josh off balance. The gust of wind was so ferocious that it blew right into the open section of the portfolio and puffed it up like a parachute even as the damaged truck kept going and headed off down the parkway.

The result was that the portfolio was, for just a second, yanked clear out of Josh's hand.

Josh let out a terrified, alarmed scream, and he lunged for the airborne portfolio, paying absolutely no attention to where he was.

He sailed right over the railing.

With certain death yawning beneath him, Josh caught the portfolio with one hand and desperately reached out to grab the railing with his other.

His frantic fingers snagged one of the support struts and he dangled there, his feet flailing.

He lasted only about two seconds, and then he lost his grip.

A hand wrapped around his fingers.

He looked up.

It was Zack Markus.

"Give me your other hand!" yelled Zack. "I haven't got a good grip! *Your other hand!"*

"I can't! I can't let it go!" He tried to bring up his other hand while still holding the portfolio, but it was big and made of leather and too awkward.

"Josh, you're slipping! Now! Now!"

He wanted nothing more than to keep holding on to it, to find another way.

Yes, Mascot died, but at least he died a hero, and maybe . . .

"Josh!" and it was his mother, and she was yelling his name, begging him to live, and Harrelson was trying to reach down to grab him, but he was at a bad angle, and Zack was losing his grip.

That was when Kelsey's voice boomed over the megaphone:

"But what Mascot knows that the others don't is that there's a duplicate of the secret plans hidden in a safe back at headquarters! So, in a brilliant scheme to fool the bad guys, he lets the plans go, knowing that they'll think the plans are destroyed but they are, in fact, safe and sound!

Another triumph for—"

"*Mascot!*" shouted Josh, and he released the portfolio. It tumbled to the parkway as he swung his now-free hand up and grabbed Harrelson's outstretched one.

Once he was in the grip of both men, it was only a matter of seconds. Hoisted as if he weighed nothing, Josh felt his sneakered feet land on the bridge. The moment he saw Kelsey, he said hopefully, "There are duplicates?"

"Of the pages? Not that I know of."

He scowled. "So you tricked me, is what you're saying."

"No, I didn't. I counted on Mascot to save Josh, because Josh is the one I care about." She smiled.

Before he could reply, he vanished into the enfolding arms of his mother, who was sobbing his name.

That was when they heard the sudden honking of cars and the screeching of tires.

"*Paul!*" It was Stan Kirby who had shouted. "*Get out of there!*"

Josh twisted away from his mother and looked over the edge of the guardrail—and his mouth dropped in shock.

Paul had slid down the embankment and was running right out into the middle of the Hutchinson River Parkway.

The portfolio had landed smack in the center lane.

Paul, paying absolutely no attention to the oncoming cars, sprinted out toward the portfolio.

The foremost of the cars hit its brakes, sliding so hard that it spun out. As if Paul had a force field protecting him, the car windmilled right around him. It skidded into the far right lane, into the path of another car, which cut hard to the side. The Hutch had no shoulder, so the far right car, an SUV, went right up onto the embankment, churning up dirt under its wide wheels.

One after the next after the next, horns blaring, cars skidded, jammed, and slid to a halt, no one wanting to proceed for fear that this apparent lunatic in the middle of the road might dash in front of them. It was all happening so fast that they didn't have a chance to figure out why he was there; they probably thought he was trying to kill himself.

Nothing could have been further from Paul's mind. Instead, very calmly, as if he were picking it up off a desk, Paul crouched next to the portfolio, straightened it out, and adjusted the artwork so that it all slid in. Then he meticulously zippered the case back up and held it aloft. "No problem, Mr. Kirby!" he shouted. "I got it!"

Then, for the first time, he noticed that there was an array of cars facing him. The air was thick with the smell of burned rubber.

Miraculously, no one had collided with anyone. That didn't seem to improve the tempers of the drivers, however, with several of them starting to get out of their cars, shouting at Paul and demanding to know what in the world he thought he was doing.

Paul raised the portfolio over his head, and in an astoundingly loud voice that carried above all the noise, he shouted, *"It's okay! Everything's under control! I work for a comic book company!"*

This odd pronouncement silenced everyone for a moment, and then the nearest driver, a man with thick glasses, demanded, "Which one?"

"Wonder Comics," Paul said proudly.

"Oh." They all looked at one another, and then the man said, "Well . . . okay, then."

CHAPTER 17

HOMECOMING

*T*hings happened quickly after that.

The police straightened out all the traffic. Doris yelled at Josh. Zack yelled at Kelsey. Both of them yelled at Paul. Stan told them to leave Paul alone. Zack yelled at Josh. Doris told him to stop yelling at her son. The sheriff told everyone to stop yelling, and then he yelled at everybody. Then he told Josh, Kelsey, and Paul that the only reason he wasn't arresting the lot of them was because Mr. Kirby asked him not to, so he wouldn't, but if any of them ever caused any trouble in Northchester again, he'd throw them in jail for ten years without even bothering with the courts, and Kelsey said she didn't think he could do that, but he said he'd find a way and he sure looked like he meant it. Stan Kirby decided to drive Paul back to Wonder Comics personally while Josh and Kelsey were taken back home by their parents.

When the car pulled up at Josh's house, Zack spoke for the first time since they had left Northchester. "I'd better come in and tell the officer that everything is okay."

"Do you think he's still here?" asked Doris, who had frankly forgotten that there had been a police officer dispatched to the house.

"It's possible. I told him he could go, but he might have stayed. It's not like I'm his boss. And it would probably help matters if the whole explanation for this came from me because, well . . . we speak the same language."

"English?" asked Josh.

"Don't start, Josh," Doris warned.

It didn't seem if Josh had even heard her. "You know, I saw this movie the other day about a guy on trial, and the lawyer says, 'Tell the jury what happened in your own words.' And if a lawyer ever said that to me, I would tell him everything in Flurbish, which is this whole language that I made up, because those would be my own words."

Zack stared at him. Kelsey sank into her seat and waited for an angry response.

To her astonishment, Zack laughed.

Really, really laughed. Laughed louder and longer than anything she'd ever heard from him since her mother died.

Doris watched, amazed, and then she smiled and shook her head at Zack's reaction.

Finally Zack managed to regain control of himself, and then he said to Doris, "He never stops."

"You get used to it," she said.

"Yeah. I guess you do. You getting used to it, honey?"

Kelsey sagged in relief. "I . . ."

"You what?"

"I thought sure you'd tell me I couldn't see Josh anymore."

Zack gave Doris a weird kind of look, then smiled and said, "It's been my experience that telling kids they can't see each other never works. On the other hand," he continued firmly, "there's going to be some serious grounding that needs to be addressed."

"Your father's right, Kelsey," Doris said.

Surprised, Josh looked from one to the other. "Did you guys go off and get married or something?"

Doris cleared her throat loudly, and Zack said, "Okay, let's go inside."

"Did you—?"

"*No!*" they chorused.

"Okay, okay!"

"Go on in. We'll be right behind you."

Kelsey and Josh hopped out of the car and headed into the house. Zack got out more slowly, as did Doris. She said to him with a degree of curiosity in her voice, "You went pretty easy on him."

"I just figured if I yelled at him again, you'd jump down my throat again."

"No. There's more to it than that," she said, a little suspicious.

Zack leaned against the car, sighed heavily, and then said, "When Josh was dangling off the bridge . . . I ran."

"Okay, so . . . ?" Then she realized what she was saying even as she said it. "Oh. You ran. I thought . . ."

"Don't get me wrong, my hip hurt like the devil afterward. I paid for it. But for that moment I forgot about everything else. I forgot I'm supposed to be in pain, that I'm limping. Nothing mattered except getting to him as fast as I could. So as crazy as he made all of us, and yes, it was all incredibly dangerous . . . I guess I owe him one for making me feel like my old self. But you didn't hear me say any of that."

"Say any of what?" she asked, wide-eyed.

"Exactly," he said with a wry smile.

They went into the house.

Officer Daniel Wiener, who had indeed left when Zack and Doris had departed for New York, had returned. He was sitting on an easy chair, munching pretzels, his feet propped up on an ottoman.

There were three other people as well: Mrs. Farber, another woman, and Terry Fogarty, the next-door neighbor. The woman Doris didn't recognize had one hand resting on Josh's shoulder. He looked extremely uncomfortable with it there.

"What are you doing here?" demanded Doris of Mrs. Farber.

"I'm sorry, Doris," Terry said. "They came back here with a court order and the policeman said I had to . . ."

"It's okay," Doris said.

Wiener, who looked as if he were watching a movie unspool, said to Zack, "So you found 'em, huh?"

"What's going on here, Danny?" asked Zack.

Wiener tilted his head toward the taller woman. "Lady's from social services."

"I'm Ellen Sanchez," she informed them. "Mrs. Farber contacted me and told me some frankly very disturbing and shocking things about young Joshua here."

"Everything's under control," Doris said.

"From what I've been led to understand, absolutely nothing is under control. Fights in school. Running away."

"Everything worked out, everyone's fine," Zack assured her.

She looked him up and down. "Are you the boy's father?"

"No."

"Then you really don't have a say in this."

"Look, lady," Zack said, his annoyance rising. "This woman is a great mother, so how about—"

"Zack, it's okay," Doris told him, putting a hand on his arm. "I can handle this."

"With all due respect, Mrs. Miller," Mrs. Sanchez said, "according to Mrs. Farber, handling this is not one of your strong suits. Joshua," she continued, cutting off Doris before she could speak, "where did you run off to? What happened while you were gone?"

"You don't have to say a thing to her, Josh," Kelsey said.

"Yes, he does, young lady, and either it will be here or we will simply be taking him back to our offices."

"You're not taking him anywhere," Doris said.

"Oh yes we will. Officer Wiener here will see to that."

Wiener shrugged helplessly. "She's got the authority to do it, Zack," he said.

"Now, Joshua . . . just tell me everything that happened. Use your own words."

"Oh no," moaned Doris softly.

"Gerb," said Josh. "Mxyzptlk. Zabagabe zabagabe zabagae. Warhoon, kreegah bundolo . . ."

"Wait, wait, wait . . . what are you doing?"

"Using my own words," Josh said innocently, and then continued, his voice becoming nasal and his pronunciation elongated, "Zeeeebignew. Flarkle mindari . . ."

"*This is gibberish!*"

"No, it's not!" Josh archly corrected her. "It's Flurbish."

"I'd *like* him to learn gibberish, but tutors are *so* expensive," Doris said.

"Do you think this is some sort of joke, Mrs. Miller?" said Mrs. Sanchez. "Clearly you don't comprehend the situation you're in. A situation that, as nearly as I can determine, is entirely of your own making as a lax, uncaring mother."

"Lady," snapped Zack, "you are so off base that you could be picked off by an armless pitcher. Danny, get her out of here," Zack said to Officer Wiener. Wiener looked conflicted, uncertain of what he should do.

Now Mrs. Farber stepped forward, waggling a finger in Doris's face. "I warned you that it would come to this, Mrs. Miller," she said severely, "but you wouldn't listen. You've no one to blame but yourself."

"Get away from my mother," Josh said heatedly.

The arguing went on for close to half an hour, until finally Mrs. Sanchez declared, "All right, this has gone on long enough. Clearly nothing is going to be settled here. Joshua, I hate to do this, but you're coming with me. Your obsession with comic books has brought you to a very unhealthy place, and the sooner you're out of this environment, the better."

Doris stepped directly into Mrs. Sanchez's path. "You take him over my dead body."

"Officer," Mrs. Farber called out, "get this woman out of our way."

"You get out of my house!"

"Happy to, but Joshua is coming with us."

"Stop calling me Joshua! It's 'Josh'! Ma!"

"Calm down, Josh. You're not going anywhere."

"Oh yes he is, and you have nothing to say in the—"

"*Pipe down!*"

None of them had spoken. It was instead a thunderous,

angry voice filled with age and authority.

Stan Kirby was standing in the doorway. He was hold-ing the portfolio under his arm. "What the blazes kind of example are you setting for these kids"—he pointed at the adults accusingly—"shouting so loud I could hear you down the street?"

"Sir," Mrs. Sanchez began, "this is none of your—"

"Shut up."

"Sir, there's no cause for . . ."

Stan strode toward her, and his presence, his energy, seemed to fill up the room. "Girlie, I'm old enough to be your grandfather, which means I'm old enough to take you over my knee and give you a good paddling for disrespect-ing your elders. Now shut your pie hole right now, savvy?"

"I—"

"*Now!*"

To the astonishment of just about everyone in the room except Kelsey and Josh, Mrs. Sanchez backed down. Mrs. Farber seemed about to protest, but all Stan had to do was fire her an annoyed look as if she weren't even worth his time.

Then he turned to Josh and, as if no one else were in the room, he asked, "How could Captain Major be Mascot's father?"

"Wh-what?"

"I said, how could Captain Major be Mascot's father, since Captain Major's been around for years and Mascot's father only just disappeared?"

There was dead silence in the room. All eyes were on Josh, who had never actually worked out the details beyond wishful thinking.

His mind raced, and then he said, "Maybe it could be like what they do in the Phantom."

"The Phantom? You mean the Lee Falk Phantom? The Ghost Who Walks?"

"Right," said Josh. "Except he's not really a ghost. It's just that when one Phantom dies, his son takes over and nobody knows that it's a whole bunch of guys. So it would be something like that. Maybe the previous Captain Major died, and Mascot's father had to become the new Captain Major." His voice became more excited in the telling. "And the reason he took Josh Mills and made him Mascot is because he's training his own son to take over after him. And he's going to reveal the secret when he's ready."

"Hunh."

Slowly Kirby walked over to the couch, and sat, looking thoughtful. "Not original in its concept . . . but the whole training-without-the-son-knowing makes a nice twist. I like it." He pulled on his chin thoughtfully. Then he unzipped the portfolio and pulled out the art boards. "I like it. A lot. In fact . . . I like it a lot better than this."

And he ripped up the art pages.

"*What are you doing?*" Josh cried out.

Slowly, methodically, Kirby continued to tear the pages to bits. "No point in doing one story when another story is much better."

Kelsey, standing several feet away, said, "But . . . what about the fan vote to kill Mascot?"

Stan Kirby snorted derisively. "Here's a tip about comics: The fans don't know what they want until they see it in front of them."

"And all the other stuff . . . about Captain Major being an outlaw and Butch Longo and—"

"We write it off. We say it was a hoax or a dream or an imaginary tale. No big deal, kid. It's comics. You'd be amazed what you can get away with. So . . . you told me you draw?"

"Yeah . . ."

"You any good?"

"He's great," said Kelsey.

"Well, we're gonna find out. I could use an assistant. I got a whole book to redraw, almost no time to redraw it in, and it's going to be late for the publisher. You're gonna have a houseguest for the next few days, Doris. You okay with that?"

"I . . . I guess, sure. . . ."

"Good. You! Officer Bob!"

"Actually," said Wiener, looking confused, "my name is—"

"I don't care. I got a case full of pencils and ink brushes, a portable draft table, and clean bristol boards in my trunk." He tossed the keys to Wiener, who caught them out of reflex. "Go get 'em."

"Sir, you can't just—"

"How about you don't give me any grief, and I'll draw you into the comic. Beef up the muscles and everything."

Wiener's face lit up. "Really?" When Stan nodded, Wiener was out the door.

Kirby got to his feet, and he turned to Doris. "Sorry I'm barging in on you like this, but I drove like a nut to get here and I sure don't have time to head back home. You got someplace Josh and I can work?"

"There's the den."

"Perfect."

"Ex . . . excuse me," Mrs. Farber finally found her voice.

"Don't even think," Stan Kirby warned her, "about

getting in the way of art. Okay, sport, let's go. Busy, busy, busy. We have to make some magic."

They set up shop in the den and, as soon as Wiener brought in the materials, got to work. They heard Mrs. Farber arguing with Mrs. Sanchez, and Mrs. Farber arguing with the police officer; that went on for a while. All during that time Stan Kirby discussed the beats of the story with Josh, and by the time Mrs. Farber marched in, Stan had already done thumbnail sketches of the twenty-two pages.

Doris was standing directly behind Mrs. Farber and saying warningly, "You lay one hand on my son and you won't be laying it on anything else for quite some time."

"Josh," Mrs. Farber said, ignoring Doris, "I've spoken to the police officer, and he's spoken to his superiors, and they all agree that Mrs. Sanchez and I are within our rights to have you go with us."

"He's my assistant and he's not going anywhere," Kirby informed her.

"Mr. . . . . whoever-you-are . . . don't you see that you're just making this worse? Comic books are what got him into all this trouble in the first place! They're having a destructive influence on his mind! They're—"

Suddenly a bright light flooded the den.

Both Doris and Mrs. Farber were startled. They turned to discover that they were staring straight into the lens of a TV camera, mounted on a cameraman's shoulder. The cameraman was a scruffy guy with a baseball cap worn backward. The light was coming from a high-intensity floodlight mounted atop the camera. Standing next to the cameraman was a smiling man holding a microphone. To his immediate right was Kelsey, and she was grinning ear to ear.

"This is Alan Jackson," she said, chucking a thumb at him. "He's a TV news reporter. I managed to get through to him at his TV station because I thought he might be interested in this."

"That," said Jackson, "is an understatement. Mr. Kirby, I'm a huge fan. And I hear that you and this young man are in the process of saving Mascot. Is that true?"

"Sure is. Don't have time to chat, though."

"You know who you should really talk to?" Doris said quickly. "This lady right here," and she put a hand on the camera and angled it so that it was pointing at Mrs. Farber. "This is Josh's guidance counselor. She was the first one to see his artistic genius. Isn't that right, Mrs. Farber?"

Mrs. Farber's mouth moved and no words came out immediately. Jackson stepped forward, putting the microphone right up in her face as he said, "Guidance counselors sometimes get a bad rap, but you obviously are a cut above the rest, Mrs. Farber. Isn't that right?"

"I . . . I guess," she stammered.

"At what point did you realize that Josh here was an artistic genius?"

"Well, he—" She cleared her throat and automatically smoothed her blouse. "He was always very imaginative. Sometimes too much so." She appeared to be rallying, although she was still forcing herself to smile for the camera. "For instance, he . . . he seemed to have trouble differentiating reality from fantasy. Even Mr. Kirby here would have to admit that everything about his comic book is a complete invention of his mind."

Jackson swung the camera back to Kirby. Stan had been drawing, but for the first time he looked nonplussed. "Well . . . now . . . if we're gonna go be completely truthful . . . I have to cop to it . . . some of the stuff in Mascot's life, I was drawing from inspiration."

"Inspiration?" asked Jackson.

"Look . . . I'm an old man," grumbled Kirby. "What do I know about kids and single moms? I was getting a lot of stuff from a blog I stumbled across. Some poor woman . . . she didn't give her own real name, although she would talk about her son, Josh, which is where I got Mascot's first name. See?" He smiled at Josh. "There are other kids in the world named Josh besides . . ."

"This blog," Doris said cautiously. "Is it written by someone who calls herself Struggling Mom 35?"

"Yeah!" Kirby said, obviously surprised. Then his eyes narrowed. "Why? You know her?"

Doris extended her hand. "Pleased to meet you. The 'Struggling Mom' is me, and the '35' is my age."

Kirby's face went slack jawed even as, reflexively, he shook her hand. "You . . . *you're* . . . the one whose blog I've been reading? This Josh . . . he's *the* Josh?"

The only one in the room who didn't look at all flummoxed was Josh himself, who, the picture of serenity, simply said, "Tol'ja so."

"So," the newsman said, unsure of whose face to thrust the microphone into, and—going for the best visual—electing Mrs. Farber's since she look the most stunned, "Mrs. Farber! You have a celebrity in your midst! Josh Miller, the inspiration for Mascot! And you were the one who recognized his artistic prowess as well! How does that make you feel?"

"Well, it . . ."

"She wanted to take me away," said Josh.

"No! No, no, not at all!" Mrs. Farber interrupted with a forced laugh, her cheeks flushed. "That was just . . . it was all a misunderstanding. Wasn't it . . . Mrs. Miller . . . ?"

"Social services is in my living room" was Doris's icy response.

"Oh! I'll get that all straightened out. Like I said, just a huge misunderstanding. . . ."

All the chatter was distracting the artists. "Could you all get the heck out of here? We're working," Kirby said.

Nobody moved.

"*Now!*" Kirby and Josh said in unison.

And miraculously, everyone else left the room.

CHAPTER 18

DANGER FROM ABOVE

The fans at the comic book convention surged forward at the autograph table as Josh and Stan sat on the other side, signing comics as quickly as they could manage.

The room was packed, and everyone was talking so loudly that it was hard to make out what any one person was saying, although curiously some of them sounded like they were saying things like "peas and carrots" or "rutabagas" over and over again. Off to one side, Kelsey, Doris,

Zack, and Paul were looking on and smiling at the public display of adoration that Josh and Stan were receiving. Daylight filtered in through a skylight in the ceiling.

Suddenly there was a loud scream. Everyone turned at once.

A man dressed as a car had burst in.

His costume was cobalt blue metal. Headlights, set to emit high beams, were mounted in a large structure atop his head, and his face was covered with grillwork. The high beams flared on, causing everyone to flinch, squinting, trying to avoid being blinded by their high intensity. He had spinning tires mounted on his shoulders and hips.

"*It's Auto Immune!*" shouted Josh. "*The race car robber!*"

Without hesitation, Auto Immune grabbed Kelsey, wrapping one arm around her throat. "Everybody stay where you are, or the girl's roadkill!"

"Let her go!" Doris shouted valiantly. "She's done nothing to you!"

"Sorry, lady, but the race is to the swift," said Auto Immune.

"*Then this is your last lap!*" came a heroic voice from above.

The skylight crashed inward, and two colorfully clad

figures dropped down from overhead. They hit the ground standing and assumed fighting poses.

"Captain Major and Mascot!" Auto Immune cried out.

"That retread is looking a little *tired*, wouldn't you say, Captain?" Mascot called out, thumping his palm with his fist.

"He certainly does, Mascot. I'd say it's time for a pit stop," replied Captain Major.

Everyone froze. Nobody moved. Nobody said anything.

"*Aaaaaaaand cut!*" came the voice of the director. "Check the gate!"

"Gate's clear," replied the cameraman.

"Excellent! Okay, let's get set for close-ups! That was perfect, everyone!"

All the people unfroze, relaxed, and then started chatting with one another. Auto Immune released his hold on Kelsey and said cautiously, "I didn't hurt you, did I?"

"Not at all." Kelsey grinned.

"It's not always easy to tell in this stupid costume."

"Hey!" snapped Kirby. "I designed that 'stupid costume.'"

"Sorry, Mr. Kirby," said Auto Immune contritely.

With the shot completed, the tech crew started rearranging the walls on the set so that the movie cameras could be moved into position. All the extras who had been playing comic book fans headed to the crafts services table, where donuts, bowls of potato chips, and other snack foods had been piled up. In the meantime the stunt coordinator was unbuckling Captain Major and Mascot from the harnesses that had been used to drop them in through the "skylight."

Once he was out, Mascot walked over to Josh, who was standing up behind the table and stretching. "How was that, Josh? Did I sound right to you?"

Josh flashed him a high sign, and the actor playing Mascot grinned.

Josh noticed that Kelsey was standing a short distance away, gazing at Mascot. He sidled over to her and said, "Admit it: Now that you see Mascot . . . he's pretty exciting."

She laughed at that. "Josh! After everything we've been through, you still don't get it, do you? You *still* don't realize how special you are. In case you didn't notice, *Mascot* came over to *you* and asked *you* what you thought of *him*. What does that tell you?"

"It wasn't really Mascot. It was an actor."

"Right." She rested her hands on his shoulders. "He was pretending to be a hero. And Mascot's adventures are made up, too. But you, Josh . . . Josh, you may make things up, but there's nothing made up about you. You get it now?"

He stared at her, considered it. "No," he said.

She sighed and then laughed. "Well . . . you will eventually."

She stepped aside as Paul ran up to them. "Hey, Josh! You were great!" he said. He and Josh high-fived, and Paul said eagerly, "So what's it like, huh? I mean"—and he gestured around the soundstage—"here they are, making a movie based on the issues that you wrote with Mr. Kirby. It must be great for you. You're really, really living in a world of comic books and superheroes now."

Josh looked toward his mother and Kelsey's dad. Zack had an arm draped around her shoulder, and they were laughing over something. That's how they'd been for some time now. Maybe getting married? Hard to know, but it was a definite possibility.

Then he looked toward Stan Kirby, who was rooting around in his portfolio case for something. Stan had become a mentor to him, praising his artwork and guiding him toward what Stan was sure would be a promising career as a storyteller.

And he thought about what Kelsey had just said.

"Oh, I dunno," said Josh. "I mean, comics are okay and

everything . . . but there's a lot to be said for real life, too."

"Ah!" Stan Kirby said, and he pulled out from his portfolio a copy of Captain Major. Josh didn't recognize the cover, though. "Thought you'd want to see this, sport. It's an advance copy of the next issue. Just to show you I can still produce issues without you."

"I never thought you couldn't, Stan. . . ."

Josh's voice trailed off. He was looking more closely at the cover.

Mascot was being passionately kissed by Large Lass with a big heart drawn around them.

Josh gulped.

Mascot's greatest challenge! How will he get out of this one?

Then he looked toward Kelsey, who was standing a short distance away. She smiled at him and winked. Josh smiled at her, and then he winked back.

Maybe this was the trap that Mascot wouldn't be able to escape. And maybe . . .

. . . maybe it wasn't such a bad thing at that.

ACKNOWLEDGMENTS

Mascot began his fictional life during a lunch meeting with two former agents of mine, Matt Bedrosian and Frank Balkin of the Paradigm Agency in Los Angeles, as a possible film story. Mascot has changed quite a bit since those early days, but that was where his masked face first popped up, and I'm indebted to those two gentlemen for Josh Miller's existence.

Also many thanks to editor Jill Santopolo at HarperCollins, whose interest in Josh, and suggestions for story direction, were instrumental in creating the final work.

The entire concept of fans voting on whether or not to kill off an annoying superhero sidekick owes its origins to DC Comics' 1988 "Death in the Family" Batman storyline, during which DC set up a 900 number and fans could call in to decide whether or not Robin (Jason Todd, not his predecessor, Dick Grayson, or his successor, Tim Drake) should die at the hands of the Joker. The fans voted to snuff him out, and so he died in an explosion. To the best of our knowledge, no actual fans named Jason Todd freaked out about it, but you never know.

Finally, "Stan Kirby" is an obvious tip of the hat to writer Stan Lee and artist Jack Kirby, who individually and together were responsible for almost every memorable Marvel Comics character created in the 1960s. Stan Kirby, however, is merely an homage to those two gentlemen, and the opinions he expresses are not intended to be an accurate reflection of how either of those two comics greats regarded either their body of work or the world of comics fans.

FOREST PARK ELEMENTARY

3XRBGOO386751Y   Fic Dav
Mascot to the rescue!

DATE DUE		

3XRBG00386751Y
Fic   David, Peter (Peter
Dav   Allen)

Mascot to the
rescue!

FOREST PARK ELEMENTARY
DIX HILLS, NEW YORK   11746

472824 01359   45349D   0004